A Bit of a

and other stories

Mary Steele was born in Newcastle, NSW, and grew up and went to school in Ballarat, Victoria. She has reviewed children's books for *The Australian*, has been a primary school librarian, and has also done freelance writing, research and tutoring. She now lives in Melbourne and divides her time between writing, visiting schools, addressing children's literature groups, gardening, craftwork and looking after her young grandchildren.

Mary won recognition with her first book for younger readers, *Arkwright*, which was voted Children's Book Council Junior Book of the Year in 1986. Critics and children alike responded to Mary's lovable eccentric Giant Anteater and the book was acclaimed as one of the finest debut novels by an Australian children's writer..

Her follow-up to *Arkwright*, *Mallyroots Pub at Misery Ponds* (1988), was applauded as a wonderful depiction of the oddness of outback life, and was judged by the *Canberra Times* to beat the film *Crocodile Dundee* hands down in the comedy stakes.

Overwhelmed by letters from her young fans, eager to find out about Arkwright's further adventures, Mary then wrote *Citizen Arkwright* (1990), applauded as every bit as funny and inventive as *Arkwright*.

Featherbys (1993)marked a new departure for Mary. Although the characters are as humorous and eccentric, *Featherbys* is a more thought-provoking read and has proved to be her most popular book so far. It has been short-listed for the CBC Awards, the YABBAs (Young Australians' Best Book Awards) and the Multi-cultural Children's Book Awards.

A Bit of a Hitch is Mary's fifth book for Hyland House.

By the same author:

Arkwright
Mallyroots' Pub at Misery Ponds
Citizen Arkwright
Featherbys

A
Bit
of a
Hitch

MARY STEELE

HYLAND ❧ HOUSE

First published in Australia in 1995 by
Hyland House Publishing Pty Limited
Hyland House
387–389 Clarendon Street
South Melbourne
Victoria 3205

National Library of Australia
Cataloguing-in-publication data:

Steele, Mary, 1930-
        A bit of a hitch and other stories

        ISBN 1 875657 58 4

        1. Children's stories, Australian. I. Title.

A823.3

Line Drawings by Virginia Barrett
Typeset in Caslon 540/Caslon Open Face by Hyland House
Printed in Australia by Australian Print Group, Maryborough,
Victoria.

Contents

Author's Note

'Aunt Millicent' was first published in *Dream Time* (Viking Kestrel 1989), edited by Toss Gascoigne, Jo Goodman and Margot Tyrrell.

'Staying with the Slingsbys' was first published in *Into the Future* (Viking 1991), edited by Toss Gascoigne, Jo Goodman and Margot Tyrrell.

I would like to thank Susan Steele for helping to solve a sticky bit in 'New Brooms', and Wendy and John Bibby for guiding me round Sandringham and for checking my description of the area in 'My Bonnie Lies Over the Ocean'.

For William Munro Steele

A Bit of a Hitch

Our family is slightly off-beat. To start with, I'm a twin. My twin brother is Matthew and I landed the name of Harriett, but we've pruned our names down to Matt and Hatt. Because we're twins people usually talk about us as if we're one person and call us 'Hattanmatt', which Mum says makes us sound like a foreign tribe or a sort of floor covering.

Being twins isn't all that peculiar, really, and at least we're not identical, but there's something else—we also have a half-brother called Hitch who is twenty-four, twice our age. We all have the same father, but Hitch has a different mother, which explains why he's only a 'half'.

Hitch's mum, who was Dad's first wife, shot through one day with a Bulgarian weight-lifter when Hitch was only eight. Dad blamed it all on the Olympics; Hitch's mum got so addicted to watching the weight-lifting contests on television that she started visiting a local weight-lifting club as a spectator to keep her going during the four-year gap between Olympics, and that's where she met Boris. Once she'd seen Boris straining and sweating and groaning and rippling his muscles, poor old Dad and Hitch didn't stand a chance.

Well, after losing out to Boris, Dad got a divorce and married our mum, and Hitch was twelve when Matt and I were born. And in spite of Matt and me being a double and Hitch being a half, we get on all right—in fact, Hitch is just as good as a whole brother and he doesn't treat us as kids even though he's old enough to be our uncle.

Hitch doesn't live at home any more, but he pays unexpected visits. Mum has a joke about them. When he's not here she says, 'Things are going without a Hitch,' but during one of his visits, or just after, she changes this and says, 'There's been a bit of a Hitch'. This was quite funny when Mum first thought of it, but she's done it to death now and we wish she'd think up a new joke.

I know what she means though—life is quite different when Hitch comes home. When he's not here, he is zooming round Australia having adventures. He started doing this as soon as he left school, and he hitchhiked everywhere until he was old enough to get his driver's licence. That's how he got his nickname. We still call him Hitch even though he now drives a battered Land Rover which he bought about fourth hand. His real name is Eric.

Hitch says he makes a living by learning to do whatever jobs people want done. He calls this 'learning new skills'. Some of the new skills he's learnt have been as a cattle drover, shearers' cook, bartender, garage mechanic, backhoe operator, abattoir hand, bean picker and fencer. When nobody wants these skills, he washes dishes or comes home.

We never know what to expect when Hitch comes home, except for the state of the bathroom. He has usually been out in the wilds and he loves to have a huge wallow after being without hot water and drains for weeks. He tries to clean up the bathroom after one of these wallows, but even Matt agrees that Hitch's standards aren't high or anywhere near it. The bath always has a sort of delta of brown or red mud in the bottom, and the handbasin under the mirror will be decorated with tufts of black hair where Hitch has been trimming his beard with Mum's dressmaking scissors, and the floor tiles will be slithery with grey slop.

The Land Rover is always filthy too, with wiper half-moons on the dust-caked windscreen and globs of dried mud on the wheels and bumpers. The interior is usually like an uncleaned birdcage, but Matt and I can never wait to see what Hitch has on board. Once he had a concussed wombat which had walked into a passing car. Another time he brought a carpet snake for company. Mum was prepared to have the wombat in the house while it was in intensive care, but it was shot out when it felt well enough to dig holes in the cork tiles. And Mum refused point-blank to make friends with the carpet snake. In the end Hitch donated it to a reptile park because the only place it would settle down in the Land Rover was twined in a huge knot round the hand brake. This made driving difficult, he said.

Well, those were the sorts of things Mum meant when she said there'd been 'a bit of a Hitch', but they were just pinpricks compared to what happened last time.

We hadn't seen Hitch for ages because he'd been up north having a look at the Daintree and the Gulf Country, and that's a fair hike from our place near Brisbane, even though it's in the same state. But late one afternoon he suddenly arrived, looking like a bushranger and smelling even worse.

'Sorry to turn up out of the blue!' he grinned. (He always did turn up out of the blue, so we weren't sure why he was sorry this time.) 'I've been going flat out for two or three days to get here—haven't had much sleep. I have to be in Toowoomba late tomorrow for a wedding, see.'

'A wedding!' exploded Mum. 'Looking like that! Whose wedding?'

'Old Dingo Duncan's—remember him? We used to drove cattle together way back, just out of school. Then he went to Uni and now he's a lawyer, the old fraud. Bet it'll be a posh wedding.'

'What are you going to wear?' Dad asked nervously.

'Aw, Dingo's got it all organised—the outfit will be waiting for me up there in Toowoomba. He's hired all the fancy gear for us.'

We all stared at him.

'What's up? Dingo knows what's what—he and I are about the same size.'

'Are you telling us that you are one of the bridal party?' Mum asked, rather weakly.

'Yeah—I'm the best man. Didn't I tell you?'

'You did not.' Mum looked grim. 'Right. As soon as you've brought your stuff in, you're going into the bathroom to remove all that tropical filth and compost from your person, no matter what it does to our drains, and this time *I'm* going to cut your hair.' Mum can be very fierce.

4

'Okay, that's great,' grinned Hitch. 'Meantime Hattanmatt can help me sort out the Land Rover.'

'Fancy arriving at a posh wedding in that old bomb,' I snorted. 'Are you going to hose it down?'

'Maybe, if there's time.' Hitch was herding us out towards the famous vehicle which, if possible, looked even filthier than its owner.

'Pooh!' complained Matt as Hitch opened up the back. 'Did you drive all the way with that stink?'

Hitch looked quite offended. 'What stink?'

I joined in. 'That ghastly stink like rotting garbage. *UGH!* What is it?' It really was awful, but Hitch must have become immune to it.

Matt was sniffing around among the chaos in the back of the Land Rover. 'It's coming from this,' he announced, poking his nose gingerly towards a large plastic tub thing which was half hidden by muddy groundsheets, a swag of bedding, blackened frying pans and other junk.

'Yeah—well, that's what I wanted to tell you about, what's in that container.' Hitch looked a bit shifty. 'I'd like you to look after it for me here while I'm in Toowoomba—just for a couple of days.'

'*That* stinking mess!' I shrieked. 'You ought to take it to the tip. Pooh! We don't want it here! What on earth did you bring it for? What is it?'

Hitch opened the front of the Land Rover and pushed us both inside. Then he leaned in and half closed the door behind him. He was behaving very strangely and the smell was atrocious.

'Listen,' he hissed. 'I've got something special in that bin, but it's best that no-one else knows about it just for now. I've been counting on you two to help me out. Trouble was I lost track of the date up north and didn't leave myself enough time to deal with this

5

properly before the wedding, so I just had to bring it with me.'

'*But what is it?*' Matt and I yelled in unison.

'Shhh!' Hitch looked solemn and his voice sank to a dramatic whisper. 'It's a clutch of croc's eggs, that's what it is.'

There was silence for a moment, then Matt's face broke into a grin.

'No kidding!' he gasped. 'But gee, Hitch—is it legal for you to have them? Crocs have been protected here since 1972, you know.'

How on earth did Matt know *that*, and how could he act so calm when I couldn't even decide whether I should be shrieking with laughter or fainting with fright? Then I remembered that Matt had done a project on crocodiles in Year 5, the time I'd done Cane Toads.

'I *know* they're protected,' growled Hitch. 'That's the problem, and I'll take the eggs to a croc farm or the zoo as soon as Dingo's wedding is over. I just need you two to mind them for me until then.'

'Where did you get them?' I had found my voice and tried to sound cool.

'Well, some hoons had been through this croc region ahead of me—they might have been poachers, or more likely just idiots. Anyhow, they had guns and they must have disturbed this old mother croc who was guarding her nest.'

I gaped. 'You mean crocodiles have *nests*, like birds?'

'Yeah, why not? They lay eggs don't they? They make this great big nest of mud and sticks near the water and the old mum buries her eggs in the mush, and the rotting vegetation keeps them warm, see?'

'So that's why it stinks?'

'I guess so. Anyway, this old mum must have had a

go at these fellows and they shot her. Seems like they panicked. They probably weren't poachers or they would have taken her skin—and they left the eggs behind, buried in the nest.'

'Why didn't you leave them there too? It would have saved all this trouble,' I sniffed. 'Not to mention the stink.'

Matt groaned. 'Don't be stupid, Hatt—*you* won't make much of a mother! The eggs have to be guarded against predators, idiot, and so do the babies when they hatch.'

'Okay, smartypants. Who said I wanted to be a mother anyway? Still, I suppose it *would* be a shame to lose the eggs after all the old girl's trouble, and being shot and everything.'

'Right,' beamed Hitch. 'That's why I brought them, see! But they need to be kept warm—it'll be a lot cooler up at Toowoomba, and besides ...'

'We know ... you can't take that pong along to a wedding,' Matt finished for him. 'Okay, I'll look after them for you even if Hatt won't.'

'Who said I won't?' I snapped. 'I don't mind as long as they're out of sniffing range and somewhere Mum won't find them. She's bound to have hysterics and call the Council or something. Remember the carpet snake?'

'I'll say.' Hitch scratched his stubbly neck. 'I've been wondering about that old tin shed behind the garage—it's got a door and nobody goes in there much, do they?'

'Just a minute.' I'd decided that I was going to be Practical, because someone had to be. 'Listen Hitch, there are things we need to know—like, how many eggs are there in that bin?'

'Thirty-five. That's all I could fit into it with a good packing of mud and stuff.'

7

'*Thirty-five*!' I fought down a twinge of panic at the thought of thirty-five potential man-eaters in our shed, and took a deep breath. 'Okay ... next question. When are they due to hatch out?' I thought this was a reasonable thing to ask.

'Haven't a clue,' said Hitch, opening the car door wider. 'Not for ages, I bet. We just have to wait for nature to take its course. You'd be dead unlucky if they hatched tomorrow.'

'Why unlucky? It'd be great!' Matt exclaimed. Then he set himself up as the Great Expert (Year 5 project standard) and asked Hitch what sort of crocodiles we were dealing with.

'The *BIG* ones,' grinned Hitch.

Matt sighed. 'I suppose you mean the Estuarine Crocodile and not the Freshwater Crocodile, which is smaller. The Estuarines are the biggest and probably the most dangerous in the world, and their eggs take about three months to incubate under normal conditions,' he recited.

'Yah—show-off!' I jeered. 'That's no help if we don't know when Mrs Croc laid them, is it, and she's dead so we can't ask her, *and* the conditions are anything but normal! I'd just like to know how we cope if we suddenly have thirty-five reptiles snapping round the house while Mum goes into shock and Dad rings the police?' I gave Hitch a steely look. 'And you're in Toowoomba!'

'I'll only be gone for two days,' he protested, 'and I bet they won't hatch in that short time—all this upheaval is bound to have slowed them down. Anyway they'll be very tiny and cute when they first pop out. Even Mum will love them.'

Thirty-five of them? He had to be joking.

Hitch backed out of the Land Rover. 'Come on, no

time to lose. I've got to get polished up for this wedding.'

We followed, drinking in fresh air, and the upshot was that while Hitch and Matt carted the smelly bin round to the shed, I went inside to distract Mum's and Dad's attention. I started a discussion about style-cutting Hitch's hair for the wedding and that really got them going. Dad suggested a close shave all over, and by the time we'd had a good argument, Hitch and Matt had come back in, looking terribly innocent.

Dad sniffed warily. 'The sooner you get into that bath, Hitch, the better,' he growled. 'The place smells like a dunghill.'

There wasn't much time to worry about crocodiles that night as we were all doing our best to turn Hitch from a frog into a prince. Mum moved in on his hair and beard with her scissors, while Matt and I gave the Land Rover a scrape and hose down by torchlight and sprayed the inside of it with lavender air freshener. Dad's contribution was shoe cleaning, a pair of black socks and a lecture about the duties of a Best Man.

When we'd finished hosing the car, Matt and I used the torch to check on the bin in the shed in case there was any action. We had to grope our way carefully around all the paint cans, flowerpots, old bed ends and other junk, until we reached the croc bin in a cobwebby corner where Matt and Hitch had hidden it behind a broken wheelbarrow. Matt and I inspected the contents of the bin closely by torchlight, and we sprinkled water on top to keep the eggs moist as Hitch had told us to. The weather was warm and humid so that the old iron shed was as good as an incubator. There was plenty of smell all right, but no sign of hatching.

9

'I wish we could *see* the eggs,' grumbled Matt, poking about with his finger.

'Hitch said we're not to uncover them or they'll get cold, so stop fiddling,' I snapped. 'You know, this mulch stuff looks pretty ancient—old Mrs Croc must have made her nest a good while ago, wouldn't you say?'

'Looks like it, but only *she* could tell us how long ago.'

'And she's dead!' we chorused. Poor old Mrs Croc—she'd left us with a time bomb!

Early next day Hitch took off for Toowoomba. He looked nearly civilised, although there was a funny white strip around the edge of his neck and forehead where Mum had trimmed his hair and he'd washed off the grime.

'See you tomorrow,' he shouted as he left the kerb. 'Should be back here by late afternoon.' He gave us a wink.

'Best wishes to Dingo!' shrieked Mum, and Dad asked Hitch for the eighth time if he'd remembered the socks and told him to behave with dignity.

We could hear the growl and rattle of the Land Rover for quite a while after it had vanished round the corner.

The rest of the day passed uneventfully, although some of the local dogs seemed to be more interested in our place than usual and several times we had to shoo three or four out of the drive.

'It must be the smell,' I muttered to Matt.

'You bet—I told you about predators, didn't I! Well, dogs and foxes are some of them. Still, they can't get into the shed if we keep the door bolted.'

Luckily Mum and Dad didn't seem to feel like gardening, as the weather was so muggy, and they didn't go near the shed. In fact they spent most of the day staring at some golf championship on television, almost as addicted as Hitch's mum was to Olympic weight-lifting.

Saturday passed and Sunday arrived. All was quiet in the shed and Matt and I began to relax as the afternoon wore on because Hitch would soon be back to take over the croc-care duties. I wasn't sure whether to be glad or disappointed—it could have been fun to have a herd of little crocs galloping round in the shed, just for a short while. I decided not to think of them all getting lost in amongst the flowerpots and piles of old sacks.

Matt had dug out his Year 5 project and he kept sneaking into his room to read it. He wanted to refresh his memory, he said. When Mum and Dad were safely glued to the next round of the golf, Matt beckoned me into his room and shut the door.

'I'd forgotten this bit,' he whispered, reading from his project. 'Listen ... "When the baby crocodiles are about to hatch, they make a yelping noise inside the shells so that the mother can uncover the eggs in the nest and help the babies out."'

Without another word we slipped out to the shed. Matt held his nose and pressed one ear to the side of the smelly bin. 'Can't hear anything,' he said.

Then I tried, but there wasn't a sound.

'Oh well,' shrugged Matt, 'Hitch will be back soon and I guess by tomorrow he'll be setting off north again and taking the eggs to a croc farm, like he said. If they start yelping in the car he ought to be able to hear them, as long as the old bomb doesn't make too much row.'

'Well, let's just hope they don't yelp tonight,

because we'll never hear them from the house and we can't camp here in the shed. We'd die of asphyxiation,' I gasped, 'like I am now!'

I backed out on to the grass and Matt followed, bolting the door. It was nearly five o'clock.

Six o'clock came and at half-past Mum (wouldn't you know) said, 'Well, it looks as if things are going to go without a Hitch! We might as well have our tea now and he can have a bite later when he arrives.'

'Weddings are a real knockout,' grunted Dad, sitting down at the table. 'He's probably still sleeping it off. Anyway, he doesn't usually let us know when he's coming—why would this time be any different?'

Matt and I slid a look at one another and began to eat.

At ten to ten the phone rang and Dad answered it. Matt and I had gone to bed, but we both bounced out to see if it was Hitch.

'Yes, that was Hitch,' said Dad, putting down the receiver. 'He's been held up in Toowoomba—the Land Rover's conked out, and he and the groomsman and the bride's brothers and somebody's uncle have spent most of the afternoon trying to locate the problem and fix it. Well, they think they've found three problems but they can't fix any of them, and it looks as if they'll have to send to Brisbane for spare parts because his Rover's such an old model. He says it could be days before he gets back here.'

Matt and I both shouted '*Days?*' before we could stop ourselves.

'What's wrong?' asked Mum, staring at us. 'It's amazing that Hitch rang *at all* to let us know. He's getting quite thoughtful in his old age. Oh well, now we can all go to bed and have a good night's sleep ... without a Hitch,' she giggled.

'Okay kids ... back to bed,' yawned Dad. 'Oh, and he said to tell you he's sorry he couldn't make it tonight.'

When all was quiet, Matt sneaked into my room and shut the door. 'It's easy for *them* to have a good night's sleep,' he hissed, 'but you know what this means, don't you?'

'Well of *course* I do! It means every extra day increases our chances of having a shedful of reptiles,' I yawned. Then I remembered that I was being the Practical one. 'Okay, Matt—you're supposed to be the expert, so ... shouldn't we be making preparations?'

'What do you mean? Like buying disposable nappies?' scoffed my idiot brother.

'Ha ha,' I groaned. 'What I actually mean is, well ... do baby crocs need to jump into deep water when they hatch? And, um ... what do they eat?'

I could tell that Matt hadn't even thought of things like that—and he'd had the cheek to tell *me* I'd make a hopeless mother!

'Hang on a tick,' he said and vanished on tiptoe to his room. He came back with his crocodile project and began rummaging through it.

'Well ... the adult crocs are carnivores and they'll eat anything up to large mammals ... and, let's see, one good meal will keep them going for weeks ...'

'Oh, brilliant! Even I know all that,' I sighed. 'Come on, what about the babies? They're not quite up to a diet of large mammals or chewed leg of tourist when they pop out of the egg, are they.'

Matt went on searching and mumbling but finally had to admit that his project hadn't actually mentioned the diet of the infant crocodile, but he thought that maybe something like small frogs might do.

'Okay. How many would each croc eat at a sitting?'

I asked. 'Look, supposing each one ate two frogs—that would be seventy frogs at one go! How are we going to keep up the supply?'

Matt looked rather amazed. 'Maybe they eat other things as well.'

'Right.' Being Practical, I found, was very stimulating. 'Tomorrow morning, if we can keep Mum out of the way, I'm going to ring the Zoo or somewhere and get some proper expert advice.'

'You are?'

'Sure. What would Hitch say if we let all his babies starve?'

'You won't say anything about us having the eggs, will you?' said Matt.

'Of course not, stupid. Go to bed.'

I couldn't sleep and felt like a spit roast rolling round between the sheets. At about 3 a.m. I crept outside with the torch to make sure there was no croaking in the shed. Not a sound.

My eyes were hot and achey, but my brain was racing. It was telling me how stupid this was, to be creeping about in the dead of night listening for crocodile croaks—almost as bad as coping with a new baby, like Mrs Wailes across the street. She was always telling us how she used to spend half the night making sure that baby Jason was still breathing, until Mr Wailes bought her a walkie-talkie monitor thing to put beside the cot.

Of course! Brainwave! That's what *we* needed—a microphone in the shed and the receiver in one of our bedrooms so that we'd hear the yelps when they started! I decided to ask Mrs Wailes if we could borrow her intercom set for a few days. Baby Jason was a big two-year-old now and they probably didn't need it. That did the trick and I fell asleep.

Mum announced at breakfast that she'd be out all the morning at a meeting. Matt signalled 'good news' by treading on my toe under the table. Dad had gone to work and as soon as we'd got rid of Mum I told Matt my idea about Mrs Wailes's intercom set.

'Do you think she'll lend it to us?' he said doubtfully. 'What will you say it's for?'

I'd already worked that out in bed. 'I'll say we're doing a holiday project on Communication Techniques—well, it's true really. The baby crocs have to communicate when they need help to get out, don't they—but I won't mention them to Mrs Wailes of course. She'd probably die of terror.'

'Okay,' said Matt. 'Let's go over now and ask her, before she goes shopping.'

Mrs Wailes was a pushover. She said she hardly ever used the microphone now because Jason slept so noisily that he kept her awake, so we were welcome to have it for a week and some day when she had more time (Jason was tipping a carton of strawberry yoghurt into the cutlery drawer just then) she'd love to hear what we'd discovered about Communication Techniques.

So Matt and I took the intercom set home, read the instructions and had it installed in no time. Luckily there was a power point in the shed, so we placed the microphone in a plastic bag on top of the croc's nest and plugged the receiver in under Matt's bed, out of sight. Matt offered to have it the first night as I'd been awake most of the night before, and after that we'd take it in turns.

While Mum was out, we flung open the door of the shed for an airing, but before we had a chance to shut the gates across the drive, next-door's great lolloping dog had bounded in and we found him scrabbling about in the corner of the shed.

'Get out! *SCRAM*, you rotten thing!' yelled Matt, and I grabbed a rake and belted the dog on the backside and sent him howling. Old Mr Johansen next door stuck his face over the fence to see what was up.

'Gorblimey, what's that stink?' he roared. 'You can't blame the dog for wanting to investigate a stink like that! Has your dad bought some fancy new kind of fertiliser?'

We acted dumb and said we didn't know anything about gardening, and Mr Johansen said that was the trouble with young people these days—they were ignorant.

'I bet we could tell the old boy a few things about crocodiles,' muttered Matt. 'If they hatch out, I'm going to stick one in his letterbox.'

'No you're not,' I said. 'It would probably die before he even found it.'

We went back to check the shed. The hatching bin looked a mess, but it was mostly just the mulch which the dog had scratched about. Down in the nest we could actually see some white shapes of eggs through the mess.

'Well, at least we can see them,' said Matt. 'We know they are actually there! Boy, we were just in time—you don't suppose the dog ate any of them do you?'

'I hope not—it's so dark in here that it's hard to tell.' I began scooping up the mulch. 'Quick! Cover them up before they get cold. It's lucky we were in time—we'll have to be more careful!'

We packed the stuff back on top and watered it, then swept the mess on the floor into the dark corner of the shed and flattened it down where the dog had been digging. After that we locked the door and went back to the house to recover. A long drink of lemonade and some cake made us feel better.

'Now, concentrate,' I said. 'Mum'll be back soon and we still haven't found out about crocodile baby food. Who shall we ring?'

We tried the Zoo six times, but the number was always engaged. The crocodile farms were all a long way north and we were a bit nervous about running up a big phone bill, so Matt suggested we try the University.

'They ought to know something,' he said, riffling through the phone book. There were columns of entries under University. 'Heck!' gasped Matt. 'How on earth do we know who to ring?'

'Start at the top and read down until we get to something that sounds as if it would know about reptiles,' I suggested.

The first entry was General Enquiries. 'Would that do?' asked Matt.

'It might—we can always come back to them, if we can't find anything better.'

'Vice-Chancellor's residence?'

'No—he wouldn't know.'

In the second column we found a section called Departmental Enquiries, and we worked our way down the list ... Economics ... Humanities ... Mathematics ... Music ... and all sorts of things, until right at the end we found ... Z for Zoology.

'That'll do!' exclaimed Matt. 'Here—it was your idea, you ring them.' He handed me the phone and read out the number of the Zoology Department.

Almost before I had time to breathe a voice was singing, 'Good morning—Zoology—can I help you?'

I sucked in some air and said, 'Er, yes ... can you tell me what newborn crocodiles eat for breakfast? ... er, please.'

It sounded stupid and I wasn't surprised to hear

Matt groaning softly, but the girl on the line just replied, 'One moment, please, I'll put you through to Dr Mangrover.'

There were a few clicks, then a gruff reptile voice said, 'Mangrover.'

By then I had taken several deep breaths and remembered about being Practical. I closed my eyes because Matt was staring at me.

'Good morning,' I said to Dr Mangrover. 'My name is Harriett. I'm a school student and I need some information for a project on Estuarine Crocodiles.'

There was a sort of snuffle at the other end and then Dr Mangrover sighed, 'What sort of information?'

'Oh, it won't take long ... could you just tell me what newly hatched crocodiles eat?' This time I was careful not to say 'for breakfast'.

Snuffle snuffle, another sigh, and finally, 'Bugs, water beetles, dragonflies, earwigs, crabs, prawns, fish, anything small that wriggles, swims, flies, hops.'

'Frogs?' I asked.

'Of course frogs,' he snarled. '*And* tadpoles.'

I was scribbling all this down because I didn't want to have to ring Dr Mangrover for information ever again.

'Is that all?' he growled.

'Just one other thing—what about water?'

I could tell from the ferocious snuffles that this was an idiot question, so I quickly changed it. 'You know, do they need to go swimming straight away?'

'Their mothers seem to think so,' muttered Dr Mangrover, and he hung up.

'What a rude man!' I gasped. 'Remind me never to study Zoology in *his* department!'

'Well,' Matt defended him, 'he was probably peering into a microscope counting cells and you went and interrupted some top-level research with your silly questions.'

'*We*'re doing important research too, trying to rear thirty-five extra crocodiles for him and his zoologists to study! He should be grateful!'

'Yes, but he doesn't know what we're doing, does he. Anyway, he told you enough.'

'I suppose so, and I suppose a tub of water will have to do to begin with—as we can't supply a full-scale river.'

'Let's see the food list,' said Matt, grabbing my memo pad. 'If we're going to start stockpiling, we'd better choose things that won't escape.'

At long last Matt was learning to be Practical too. We studied the list.

'Well, my choice out of that lot would be tadpoles,' I decided. 'They can be kept fresh in a tank, and besides, we know some good places to catch them in round here.'

'And some might turn into frogs while we're waiting,' added Matt.

We spent the next two days stockpiling tadpoles from round about the district. We didn't have to explain this to Mum and Dad as they'd grown used to our tadpoling expeditions over the years. If they'd looked in the shed, though, they might have wondered why we'd filled eight old buckets and cans with about four million—the water was thick with the little black wrigglers and we hoped they wouldn't start eating each other before the crocs got a chance.

We were so busy rushing from one pond to another on our bikes that the two days flew past and only occasionally did we remember to check the hatching bin. There was no sign of life or croaking and at night all we could hear on the intercom were possums thumping on the shed roof now and then.

By Wednesday we couldn't think of any other preparations to make, and we began to realise that Hitch must arrive back soon—and still those eggs hadn't hatched. Blooming old nature was being awfully slow taking her course.

'Stupid eggs,' moaned Matt. 'I bet they're all duds! Hitch should never have moved them—it's all been a waste of time.'

I stared at the bin. We'd become used to the smell now and used to the idea of having a family of baby crocs in our shed. I didn't care if it was illegal or if Mum hit the roof—I really wanted it to happen, *here*, at our place.

Hitch arrived with a roar and a lot of tooting on Thursday morning. Dad was at work and Mum had gone to do the weekly shopping, so we were able to talk.

'Has anything happened yet?' was Hitch's first question, as he climbed out of the Land Rover.

'Not a thing,' muttered Matt. 'We reckon they're all addled—and we've been to no end of trouble too, and had sleepless nights!'

We led Hitch to the shed and showed him the intercom and the rows of tadpole buckets and the old tub we'd found for a makeshift pool. And we told him about keeping the dogs away and ringing awful Dr Mangrover and about nosey Mr Johansen next door.

'Well, good on you both!' beamed Hitch. 'It won't be your fault if they don't hatch. You've done a terrific job!'

'How's the Land Rover?' I asked gloomily. I didn't really care much, but I wanted to stop thinking about the crocodiles.

'It's in great shape, with all its new bits,' enthused Hitch. 'Should keep me going for ages. In fact I think I'll just load her up now and get on the road—I want to try and make that croc farm by tomorrow and get those eggs settled in. I don't much fancy them all hatching out when I'm driving up the highway!'

'Gee, no—that could be tricky,' said Matt, almost grinning.

'Aren't you going to stay and see Mum and Dad?' I asked. 'They'll be disappointed—they want to hear about Dingo's wedding and everything.'

Hitch looked awkward. 'Um, yes—I know. Tell you what, I'll try and come back in a few weeks and stay for a bit. But just now I must get to that farm—anyway, it'll be much simpler if we can load everything aboard without Mum being here to ask questions. And look, I might take some of those tadpoles—just in case. The croc farm can use them anyway, I guess.'

Matt and I chose the fattest tadpoles and put them in the two biggest buckets, then tied sheets of strong polythene over the top and skewered holes in them for air. Then we helped Hitch to load the egg bin into the Rover, plus all his other gear. He fished about in one of his bags and produced Dad's black socks, dirty of course.

'Say thanks from me—the socks looked great!' said Hitch. 'See you soon—wish me luck!' And with a roar and a rattle, he was gone.

Matt and I just stood there by the gate. We could hardly believe the last few days had ever happened. Now there was nothing left, no suspense, no excitement, nothing to look forward to. It had all come to an end so suddenly. I felt hollow with disappointment, hollow except for a dull ache somewhere in my middle. We mooched round to the back of the house.

'Oh, come on,' shrugged Matt. 'We'd better get rid of the rest of those rotten tadpoles before they start a frog plague in the garden.' So we carted them back to the nearest pond and tipped them in. Then we cleaned and packed up the Intercom and returned it to Mrs Wailes. She flew to the door.

'Oh hello, Hattanmatt, did you make some interesting discoveries about—whatever was it—Communication Techniques?' she asked.

I was just about to say 'No—none at all', when there was a crash and Mrs Wailes couldn't wait to listen. Jason had been trying to climb up the standard lamp. Looking after baby crocs would have been a cinch compared with looking after baby Jason.

The last days of the holidays were dreary and we were almost glad to go back to school. After a couple of weeks had passed we'd not exactly forgotten the crocodiles but we'd grown used to the disappointment, and we'd convinced ourselves that the eggs were addled anyway.

There hadn't been a word from Hitch. Mum and Dad had been quite cross that he'd dashed off like that, without staying even one night. 'And after all we did to smarten him up, too,' said Mum. 'I suppose we haven't the slightest idea where he's gone to this time, have we?'

'Back north, he told us,' mumbled Matt. 'That's about all.'

Then a postcard arrived addressed to Matt and me. On the front was a photo of the Paradise Crocodile Farm and on the back was a message from Hitch:

On Friday 14th, safely at The Farm, to the late Mrs C. O'Dile, 31 babies all doing well. Grateful thanks to Hattanmatt for expert pre-natal care and about 750 frogs. Cheerio Hitch.

'Wow!' gloated Matt. 'Thirty-one!'

'Yes, wow! Hitch said there were thirty-five to start with. There must have been four duds.'

'Probably ... unless that rotten dog ate them!'

'Ugh. Anyway, thirty-one is pretty amazing!'

We beamed at each other.

Of course Mum and Dad were frantic with curiosity. It was a nine days' wonder to get a card from Hitch.

'*Well* ?' they both bleated.

There was no reason now not to tell them, so we handed over the message.

Dad looked bewildered. 'What's it mean? ... Is this some mad joke?'

'Right—*what's* been going on?' demanded Mum. 'What in heaven's name do you two know about pre-natal care, and *who's* had thirty-one babies?'

So out came the whole story, and now we realised that it hadn't been a waste of time at all, even though we had missed out on the hatching, for maybe without us those little crocs wouldn't have made it.

'Why ever didn't you tell us?' cried Mum.

'Well ... because we thought you'd scream and ring the police. You didn't like the carpet snake, remember?'

'Well, who would? Snakes are loathsome—they don't have legs and they slither,' Mum shuddered, 'but I've heard that baby crocodiles are quite cute.'

'That's what Hitch said you'd say, but we didn't believe him,' I gaped.

Dad was looking panicky. 'I think they're much better off up there at the Paradise Farm where they have all the proper crocodile facilities,' he said, loudly. 'Really I do!'

Dad was right, of course. He was being Practical now. But ... what a major event it would have been if they'd hatched in our shed. Like when babies are born in taxis on the way to hospital—they're the ones who get their pictures on the news! I'd decided that you need a bit of unprogrammed chaos sometimes to liven things up, especially when you live in the suburbs.

Later that afternoon Mum went into the shed to find some flowerpots. We could hear her bumping about in there, moving things, saying 'Phew, what a stench!'— when suddenly there was a piercing scream!

We all rushed. 'What's the matter? Is there a snake?'

Mum backed out, shaking. 'Something ran over my foot. Not a snake ... it had feet. Like a *RAT*.'

Matt vanished into the dark corner, searching about. Then we heard thumps and scrabbling noises and then 'Gotcha!' Matt, covered in cobwebs, came to the door. 'Boy!' he breathed, '*LOOK*!' He was holding two shining, spotted, perky, wriggling reptiles, two baby crocodiles with long tails. They were perfect!

Mum thought so too. Her eyes were shining. 'They really *are* cute!' she gasped. They're darlings!'

Dad was looking weak. 'I don't believe this,' he groaned. 'Not in *our* shed. We'll be arrested!'

I rushed into the house and grabbed a big torch. 'There might be two more,' I yelled as I came back and began flashing the light around the dirt floor of the shed. In the dark corner were the remains of two eggshells lying half-buried in a mound of loose earth and rubbish. There was nothing else.

'I bet I know what happened,' panted Matt, who was having trouble holding on to his wrigglers. 'I bet Johansen's dog buried these two eggs and ate two others just before we found him.'

'Never mind what happened *then*,' snorted Dad. 'What are we going to do with them *now*, for heaven's sake? How quickly do they grow?'

'Aw Dad, don't be a wimp! They take *years*!'

24

Mum's maternal instincts were surging. 'Quick, dear,' she said to Dad. 'Help me fill this tub with water before the little pets dehydrate. Come on—hurry!'

'Yes, hurry!' shouted Matt. 'They're getting snappy!'

When the tub was filled and out on the lawn, Matt plunged the baby crocs into their bath where they turned on a dazzling display of water ballet.

Dad was groaning again, Mum was saying, 'They really are delightful!' and Matt was beaming like a sun lamp. It was left to me to be Practical, as usual.

'*FOOD*!' I shrieked. 'Quick Matt, we'll have to go tadpoling all over again.' And to think of the millions we'd tipped back!

And Mum said, 'That postcard—didn't it have the Paradise Farm's phone number on it? Now, I think we should enjoy our babies for a week or so, and then have a nice long weekend delivering them to the Farm and meeting all their brothers and sisters. Wouldn't that be marvellous fun! And we might even catch up with Hitch too! I'm sure he'll be hanging around—he's probably learning new skills as a crocodile farmer. Oh, it's all very exciting!'

Poor Dad—first weight-lifters, now this. Still, even he would probably admit that life would be pretty boring if it always went without a Hitch.

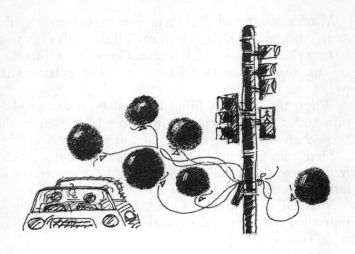

The Crossing

When old Mr Prout died, Mrs Prout decided to find a job. She had a good cry first, of course, because she and Mr Prout had been married for forty-five years and she had nursed him night and day through his last illness, managing to keep herself cheerful and strong for him. She didn't at all fancy being a widow now, and she cried on and off for three weeks after Mr Prout had gone.

But Mrs Ivy Prout wasn't one to mope. 'I'll find an occupation, that's what I'll do,' she promised herself. 'Just something to take me out into the world most days so that I won't turn into a miserable turnip.'

Whenever she found herself sighing, she would slap one hand with the other and say, 'Enough of that, Ivy Prout!'

Mrs Prout consulted the Jobs Vacant page in the local paper.

Reliable Ladies urgently needed for ironing, cleaning, baby-sitting, light household duties, etc.

Mrs Prout sniffed quite fiercely. 'That's not what I had in mind at all. I've been reliable at all those things for forty-five years and now I want to be reliable at something different.'

She read on.

Early morning Newspaper Throwers (own car or motor-bike required).

'Well, at my age I'm not keen on really early mornings, and besides I don't have a motorbike.' Mrs Prout didn't have a car either, having never learnt to drive.

Saxophone players required for new band.

Mrs Prout didn't play an instrument and she certainly didn't understand that ear-splitting noise they called music these days.

Nor did she understand what *Data Processing* was or how to be a *Word Processing Operator*. 'How do you process words?' she wondered. 'Do you put them through a mincer or slice them up or roll them out flat, like pastry?'

Mechanics, Bartenders, Junior Typists—nothing seemed suitable.

Mrs Prout had worked as a nursing sister in her younger days, but now she was well over retiring age. In any case, she had just nursed Mr Prout into his grave and she didn't want to be reminded of that any more. She needed a change.

School Crossing Supervisors required for the new
school term. Suit active pensioners, housewives/hus-
bands, etc. Applicants should be fit and healthy.

Mrs Prout stared at the advertisement. '*That* might be
it,' she thought. 'What do you think, Petunia?' she
said to the cat. 'It would get me out twice a day and I
could do my bits of shopping on the way home. And
I'd meet all sorts of people on the crossing, young
people, and I'd see the world go by.'

When she rang the number mentioned in the advertisement, she was asked to go to the local Council
Office for an interview. It was forty years since Mrs
Prout had been for a job interview and she felt a little
fluttery as she arrived at the municipal buildings and
pushed her way through the heavy swing door. She
followed the signs and found the department she
needed.

The young man who attended to her was called
S.Tank, according to a label which stood on the counter
in front of him. 'What an unfortunate name!' Mrs
Prout thought to herself. 'I wonder what he was called
at school?'

S.Tank surveyed her through his black-framed
spectacles and said, 'Good morning.'

'I've come about the school crossing job,' Mrs Prout
explained. 'I'd like to try it.'

'Ah, I see,' responded Mr Tank, noting Mrs Prout's
snow-white hair. 'I'm not sure that there are any suitable crossings left.'

'Suitable?' Mrs Prout stiffened. 'What do you mean,
young man?'

Mr Tank wasn't in favour of being called 'young
man', although he was only twenty-four. 'Well you

28

see, Madam, some crossings are less demanding than others and they are always snapped up first. The harder ones take longer to fill.'

'What do you mean—harder?'

'It's quite simple, really. A big school near a busy road makes for a harder crossing to manage than a small school on a quiet street.'

'Ah yes, I understand what you mean,' nodded Mrs Prout. 'Well, I am quite willing to try a hard one. It said the job was suitable for active pensioners, and that is what I am.'

Mr S. Tank looked solemn. 'That's as may be, but we try to allocate the easier crossings to our ... er ... more senior applicants and give the hard ones to younger persons.'

'You mean that I'm too old, is that it?' sniffed Mrs Prout. 'Well, I'm only sixty-nine and I still have my own teeth.'

Mr Tank took a step backwards in case Mrs Prout's teeth started snapping. He sensed that she wasn't going to give up without a fight.

'Madam, have you had any experience of children en masse?' he asked.

'I've had five myself, now rather far-flung, and there are twelve grandchildren,' Mrs Prout came back at him. 'Are you a father, Mr Tank?'

Mr Tank wasn't, so he changed his approach.

'Supposing there were an accident on or near your crossing. Would you be able to handle it?' he asked piously.

Mrs Prout pounced. 'Young man, I was a trained nursing sister before you were born. I have seen and coped with more accidents and blood in casualty wards than you could even imagine—arms and legs chopped off, bodies run over by trucks, heads split open like melons. I wouldn't faint, if that's what you mean,' she concluded, 'and I would know what to do.' She was pleased to see Mr Tank become pale and sweaty.

He decided to seek a second opinion. 'Excuse me a moment,' he said to Mrs Prout as he backed away hastily in search of a colleague.

The colleague reminded Mr Tank that reliable crossing supervisors were in short supply because the hours were inconvenient. 'If she's been a nurse, she should be able to keep her head, and if she can't cope she'll probably give the job away quick smart,' was the colleague's advice. 'Offer her a trial run for a month. How about that crossing in the dip on Valley Road? That's near where she lives, and it's a real hard one. That'll test her out.'

Mr Tank conveyed this offer to Mrs Prout, told her to come back in a few days time for a briefing session and a uniform, and she returned home in high fettle.

The Valley Road crossing was more than a hard one—it was a brute. Its zebra stripes lay across a busy trunk road at the lowest point of a dip between two hills. Traffic roared downhill from either direction, gathering murderous momentum for the uphill climb on the other side, and the squeal of brakes was commonplace as the pedestrian lights snapped red against the oncoming cars and trucks. Two schools used the crossing and so did people in the adjacent shopping strip, but nobody liked it. They wouldn't cross that lunatic road unless they had to. What had once been a peaceful and friendly shopping centre was now divided by a howling torrent of vehicles.

At the end of her first day as the Valley Road School Crossing Supervisor, Mrs Prout went home, sat heavily in her armchair with a powerful cup of tea, rested her legs on a pouffe, and told the cat all about it.

'Well, Petunia,' she sighed, 'speaking medically, I would describe myself as being in a state of shock—mild shock, anyway.' Petunia sat motionless.

'You couldn't imagine the number of semitrailers, delivery trucks loaded with bricks, petrol tankers, concrete mixers, mobile cranes, horse floats and refrigerated trucks full of yoghurt or pizzas, not to mention all the ordinary cars and buses. And the NOISE ...! Mind you,' Mrs Prout continued, 'I didn't lose any pedestrians. There weren't even any close shaves. Those school kiddies were very well behaved—no jaywalking or trying to beat the lights. There's no future in trying to beat those Valley Road lights, is there. You'd be mincemeat under a semi, we all know that, and the children know it too.'

Petunia's eye-slits glinted briefly at the mention of mincemeat, and Mrs Prout pondered a while as she sipped her brew of tea.

'I suppose that's one thing in favour of Mr Tank's hard crossings—pedestrians are too scared to take risks. I expect on those easy crossings you'd have stupid ninnies darting in and out of the traffic, taking no notice of the supervisor, which in some ways would make easy crossings harder than the hard ones.'

Mrs Prout closed her eyes and visualised herself in a white coat and red sash stepping out across the zebra stripes with her lollipop pole raised high, bringing the monsters to a throbbing, menacing halt, and being glared at by impatient drivers with their feet trembling on accelerators.

'Fancy, just me and my pole holding up all those huge things in both directions!' she marvelled. 'It's like Moses and the Red Sea in the Bible!'

For a moment Mrs Prout lost herself in the story she'd known since childhood, of the Israelites escaping from slavery in Eygpt and being pursued by the Egyptian Pharoah and his soldiers in their thundering chariots right to the edge of the Red Sea. And then the miracle! Moses, the leader of the Israelites, stretched forth his hand over the sea and the waters rolled back to the left and the right like walls, leaving a dry path across, so the Israelites were able to escape to the other side!

Mrs Prout opened her eyes.

'That's what it's like down there in Valley Road at my crossing, Petunia. There's a wall of growling trucks and petrol tankers and semitrailers banked up on either side, and all these children walking across between them, with just me and the traffic light to keep them safe!'

Then Mrs Prout remembered the next part of the story when Moses stretched forth his hand again, after his people were safely across, and how the waters of the Red Sea crashed back over the pursuing Egyptians and drowned them, every one.

'Dear me,' she gasped. 'It was all very well for Moses, but it just shows how careful I'll have to be not to stretch forth my hand at the wrong moment!'

Petunia yawned and curled up for a sleep.

Mrs Prout quickly realised that working conditions were rather bleak down there at the crossing, quite apart from the peril of traffic. For one thing, she didn't think that she should have to sit on a low wall while waiting for pedestrians to arrive. It was a well-known medical fact that sitting on cold, hard stone did one's posterior no good at all. So one afternoon she asked a neighbour to drive her to the crossing carrying various improvements in the boot of the car. These, when unloaded, included a canvas director's chair and a small blue-and-white striped beach umbrella which could be clipped to the back of the chair. Mr Prout had used them in his garden. The chair needed tethering in case the umbrella carried it away in a wind gust, so Mrs Prout tethered it to a post at the end of the wall. At night Mr Thrower, who ran the newsagency beside the crossing, was happy for Mrs Prout to fold up her furniture and stow it in a quiet corner of his shop behind the condolence cards.

Mrs Prout found that people stopped to talk to her now that she had a chair and a striped umbrella, whereas she had been ignored when sitting on the wall.

'You see, Petunia,' she explained during her nightly report, 'people like to be cheered up. The umbrella and the chair make the crossing seem more friendly.'

The faces of the children were becoming familiar to her and she began to learn some of their names. One afternoon a boy called Jake told Mrs Prout that next day would be his seventh birthday, and after the rush hour she sat in her director's chair for a while and pondered. When she went into the newsagency to put her things away, she and Mr Thrower had a conference.

Next morning, Mrs Prout was on the job earlier than ever. Out came her chair and her umbrella, out came two large balloons, blue and white, which Mr Thrower helped her to tie to the traffic light pole, and out came a large cardboard sign with

HAPPY BIRTHDAY JAKE!

written on it in vivid orange letters. She and Mr Thrower decided to sticky tape this to the pole on the other side of the road, so that both ends of the crossing looked jolly.

'Well, Mrs P.,' said Mr Thrower. 'I'd say you're starting something here!'

'Very likely,' she agreed—and she was.

The following day it was

HAPPY BIRTHDAY ALEXANDER & MICHELLE!

and on the third day

HAPPY BIRTHDAY STEFAN, BETTY, NATHAN, LUKE & LAVENDER!

Mr Thrower set to and made a large wooden sign with space for detachable names and a strong hook for hanging it to the traffic light pole. He was doing a spanking trade in balloons and birthday cards, so he was more than happy to assist Mrs Prout in her enterprise.

When nearly two weeks had passed and no resignation had been received at the Council Office from Mrs Prout, Mr Tank decided to investigate. He drove to work one morning along Valley Road, although it was his least favourite route and well out of his way. He didn't want Mrs Prout to recognise him, so he wore dark glasses and a tweed cap pulled well down, and he hoped that he didn't look like the getaway driver in a bank hold-up.

Surrounded by groaning semitrailers and coughing diesel trucks, Mr Tank crested the hill for the descent to the Valley Road crossing. There were many stops and starts and the air was filled with fumes and the roar of revving engines. As he neared the bottom of the hill, Mr Tank's eyes widened. He removed his dark glasses to be sure that his vision wasn't impaired—but no, there were *balloons* tied to the traffic lights.

'It must be a sales gimmick,' he decided, but then he spotted the birthday sign on the other pole.

HAPPY BIRTHDAY
AMY, DOUGAL, BRADLEY, LUIGI
& MRS SMITHERS!

'What the heck!' muttered Mr Tank. The striped umbrella and the chair next caught his eye and, yes, there was a blue bucket full of flowers standing on top of the low wall nearby—daffodils and plum blossom. Two ladies were putting up a trestle table beside the wall and, as he watched, they covered it with a blue plastic cloth and stuck up a sign announcing a produce stall in aid of the local kindergarten, opening for business at 10 a.m.

Pedestrians were congregating in large bunches at either end of the Valley Road crossing. Mr Tank tried to concentrate on his driving as he came up to the zebra stripes. The lights turned red again and he found himself in the front line, with a milk tanker hissing to a halt beside him.

Mr Tank pulled his cap down even lower and turned up his collar as Mrs Prout strode forth bearing her lollipop pole before her like a battle standard. She ushered her regiments of children across, making them keep to the left and forbidding them to run. She smiled at them and glared at the trucks, and before retreating to the footpath she approached the milk tanker and tapped on the driver's window with her lollipop.

'What's up lady?' he asked, winding it down.

'I've been watching you, driver,' said Mrs Prout sternly. 'Every day you come through here at peak time.'

'Yeah—and what if I do? This is my route.'

'It is not exclusively *your* route, driver,' Mrs Prout pointed out, 'but you come down that hill as if it were, like a thunderbolt, trying to beat these lights, and I can tell you that as long as you behave like that and as long as I am in charge of the crossing, the lights are going to beat you—every time!'

The tanker-driver's eyes popped. 'Listen lady—I have a deadline to meet! This milk has to get to the factory, no matter what *you* say.'

'If you're not more careful, you'll meet your deadline right here—and it'll be a line of dead pedestrians.' Mrs Prout banged her lollipop stick on the crossing. 'If I had my way, I'd ban that *deadline* word from the language—it causes nothing but trouble! Now, off you go and please try to drive intelligently. Your milk will get to the factory faster that way.'

Applause broke out among the pedestrians and several car horns tooted their approval as Mrs Prout plodded back to the footpath. The blushing tanker driver ground his gears as he made his escape, and Mr Tank drove forward very carefully indeed, saying 'Phew!' to himself. From the corner of his eye he saw Mr Thrower tying another bunch of balloons to a traffic sign.

Next morning Mrs Prout kept a watchful eye on the hilltop for the appearance of the milk tanker and, as it came towards her, she stretched forth her hand over the Walk/Wait button, ready to summon up a red light. But the tanker came downhill sedately, not urging or overtaking or belching fumes, and it reached the bottom at quite a gentle pace. Mrs Prout beamed and waved the bashful milkman through before pressing the button, and then turned her attention to a readymix concrete truck which was squealing to a halt at the line. Out she strode to shepherd her children across. Then, tap tap on the driver's window with her lollipop ...

Each day, Mrs Prout selected road-hogs in this way and made an example of them in front of their fellow drivers and the crowds of grinning pedestrians. Many children began leaving home early so as to have five minutes fun at the Valley Road Crossing before running on to school, and they watched the oncoming traffic with hawk-eyes, trying to pick Mrs Prout's victims.

'I bet it'll be that mobile cherry picker—see, just coming over the top now!'

'Nope—that petrol tanker is more like. It could blow up the whole shopping centre if it turned over.'

When an ambulance or fire brigade siren was heard approaching, Mrs Prout was at her magnificent best, stopping everything in sight with red lights and stern commands, then waving the screeching vehicle through the gap with great swoops of the lollipop. And, when her duties with the school children were finished, she would sit under her umbrella and watch the world go by, occasionally helping people with prams or heavy loads to operate the lights and seeing elderly pedestrians safely across.

And so, when the four weeks of Mrs Prout's trial period were up there was no question of removing her from her post. She was, in fact, already regarded as the champion crossing supervisor in the region, and Mr Tank at the Council Office preened himself and took all the credit for having appointed her. She was thought to be a miracle worker, for she had achieved what no road safety campaign or police traffic squad had managed to do: she had transformed the Valley Road's howling torrent of traffic into an orderly, smooth flowing stream, and the many regular drivers waved to her each day as if to their own dear old grandmother.

'You see, Petunia,' she explained one evening, 'there's something about us grandmothers. I have only to wag a finger and say "tut, tut" and these big tough truck drivers turn to jelly and do just what I ask!'

The Valley Road shopkeepers agreed amongst themselves that business was picking up, and the two halves of the community began to knit together again as people felt safer crossing the road. The striped umbrella had become a village centre, a small, bright oasis in a grey, concrete wasteland.

'Do you know anyone who wants a kitten?' a small girl asked Mrs Prout one day. 'We have one black and two marmalade.'

'Why not write a little notice, dear,' suggested Mrs Prout, 'and stick it on my wall there, and I'll let you know if anyone is interested.'

Soon the wall was dotted with cards and Mrs Prout found herself operating an exchange. Some people had things to give away, like a glut of tomatoes or figs, or free firewood from an old fence, while others were looking for empty jam-jars or bagpipe lessons or a recipe for pickled walnuts. Mrs Prout almost adopted a marmalade kitten herself, but decided that Petunia was too set in her ways and would be extremely upset. 'I'll wait until a canary is on offer,' Mrs Prout decided.

On her seventieth birthday Mrs Prout rose, wished herself many happy returns, enjoyed early phone calls from her far-flung family, and then set off to the crossing. 'It's business as usual, Petunia,' said she, as she whisked the cat out of the door.

But this wasn't quite the case, for when she reached the crossing she found it gorgeously arrayed with balloons of every colour and with buckets of flowers along the wall. Her umbrella was already in place and there were signs at each end of the crossing.

HAPPY BIRTHDAY
MRS PROUT
FROM VALLEY ROAD!

Children and shopkeepers were gathering to wish her well, and drivers, when they saw the signs, tooted or called their greetings as they passed through.

'Isn't this grand!' exclaimed Mrs Prout. 'How kind you all are—but how did you know it was my birthday?'

'I rang the Council Office,' said Mr Thrower. 'I guessed they'd have your date of birth on their records. Mind you, they wouldn't tell me at first—said it was an official secret—but when I explained the reason they agreed to disclose the day and the month, but not the year. So it's still half an official secret!'

'What nonsense!' sniffed Mrs Prout. 'I don't mind anyone knowing that I'm seventy years old today, yes, threescore years and ten. According to the Bible I've had my innings, but actually I feel younger now than I did two years ago. I'm not giving up yet! Now, come on children, you'll all be late for school.'

Mrs Prout pressed the Walk/Wait button, took hold of her lollipop and strode on to the crossing.

The damage was done, not by a heavy transport, but by a shabby sedan with a P plate. It careered down the hill to beat the lights, ... too late, the lights had flashed to red. The driver stamped on his brakes but his foot hit the floor. *Squeal* ... *THUD*. Mrs Prout was flung heavily across the zebra stripes, where she lay still with her lollipop pole smashed beside her.

After a frozen moment of silence, people started wailing and running and Mr Thrower dashed to ring the ambulance, the ambulance which Mrs Prout had so often guided through her crossing.

Someone helped the sedan-driver across to the wall, where he sat among the flowers, shaking and blubbering. 'I didn't mean to ...' he cried. 'The brakes just weren't there ... I dunno why ...'

'Stupid young fool,' someone muttered.

A screaming siren heralded the ambulance, which threaded its way through the piled up traffic. Quickly the ambulance officers examined the crumpled mound that was Mrs Prout.

'Okay, there's still a good pulse,' said one. 'I think it's mainly shock and bruising ... she's slightly stunned. Looks as if her pole caught the full impact and tossed her with it. Let's get her to hospital, quick smart.' With expert care they placed the old lady on a stretcher. Her white hair glowed above the blanket.

The young P-plate driver drew in a shuddering breath. 'She looks just like my Gran,' he whimpered.

'Stand back please,' commanded the ambulance driver. Many of the children were crying and truckies had climbed out of their cabins, all deadlines forgotten. One of the birthday cards had fallen sideways on the pole and the balloons bobbed stupidly in the breeze.

As the two men lifted the stretcher, Mrs Prout stirred and opened her eyes. 'What's happened? Are the children all right?'

'It's okay, Mrs P. The kids are safe.' The ambulance man patted her shoulder. 'We'll get you to hospital in a jiffy now, and they'll look after you. Everything's going to be just fine.'

'You're good boys,' Mrs Prout whispered. 'I'm sorry to be so silly.' She closed her eyes, then opened them again. 'Oh dear—would you remind Mr Thrower about the birthday list? I'm sure he'll see to it until I get back.'

The ambulance man looked round and Mr Thrower, who was hovering anxiously nearby, said, 'Of course I will. You just relax and get better, Mrs P.'

Mrs Prout's eyes were drooping again, but she had one more request. 'Please could someone give Petunia her tea? She likes it at six o'clock.'

Lulu

Ms Shirley Brown lived in a three-bedroom unit. She had converted the third bedroom into an office, which she preferred to call her Brown Study, and in there she did work for a publishing firm.

There were four units in the L-shaped block. Shirley Brown's was No.4, the back one forming the foot of the L, while the other three lined up along the driveway to the front. Behind No.4 there was a narrow garden strip which Shirley Brown called her breathing space. It was not much more than grass and a clothes line, for she had never been a green-fingered person, but she liked to loll there on a chaise longue on summer evenings, reading and sipping homemade cumquat brandy. On really hot days she would sling

an Indian bedspread across the clothes hoist to provide an exotic patch of shade.

Shirley Brown was the favourite aunt of all her
nephews and nieces. The title of 'Aunt Shirley' didn't
suit her at all and 'Auntie Shirl' even less. In any case
there was another Aunt Shirley in the family whom
the more disrespectful children called 'Burly Shirley'
on the quiet, and it wouldn't have done to confuse
Shirley Brown with *her*. So the nephews and nieces
called Shirley Brown the Brown Aunt.

She claimed to know very little about children, having none herself, so she found it simplest to treat them
as people of her own age and to offer them delicacies
like smoked trout or sips of the cumquat brandy,
which she considered to be much more civilised (and
better for them) than chips and Coke.

The eldest niece was Frances and she became the
object of widespread envy when she left the remote
family farm at the age of twelve to go to school in the
city. The envy welling up in the smaller nieces and
nephews arose not from Frankie's dazzling leap into
high school, but from Brown Aunt's offer to have her
to stay at Unit No.4 during term time.

Frankie's mother was at first nervous about this
offer, as she was not sure that her sister Shirley was a
suitable guardian for an innocent country girl.

'She'll turn the child into an alcoholic—probably
serve up cumquat brandy for breakfast instead of
orange juice,' she groaned. 'I doubt if she knows the
difference.'

Frankie's father was more optimistic. 'Let's give it
a term's trial, eh?' he coaxed. 'You know we can't
afford a boarding school, and Frankie seems happy
enough to risk her life with Shirley. Your sister's not
really a raving nut case, you know—just a bit original.'

It probably comes from living alone like that—it might do her good to have a kid to cope with for a bit.'

Frankie's mother felt a little more hopeful when she saw Brown Aunt's preparations in the second bedroom. Sensible things had been provided for Frankie, such as a small desk with a nifty little reading lamp, an empty bookcase, a bright green beanbag, and a cork pinboard above the desk.

'That's so you won't ruin my walls, darling,' said Brown Aunt to Frankie. 'I know how *essential* it is to pin things up.' Indeed, one whole wall in her own Brown Study was a giant pinboard smothered in recipes, postcards from globetrotting friends, publishing blurbs, cuttings, posters, family photos, and notices scrawled to herself in purple or green texta reminding her to put out the garbage on Mondays or to have the car serviced *without fail*.

She had hung two fairly large framed prints in Frankie's room. Facing the window was a scene of a hillside. On a background of warm, parched colours the painter had added little swirls and coils of grey and brown, with delicate strokes of white and charcoal, and as you stood back from the picture, the swirls and strokes changed magically into gum trees and rocks. Frankie could very nearly smell the sunbaked earth and the tang of ants.

Brown Aunt gestured towards the painting. 'That's a Fred Williams, darling, to remind you of home when you get too depressed by suburbia.'

Frankie liked the Fred Williams, but her father was gaping at the other picture. 'And what's this, then?' he enquired.

Three strange figures seemed to be dancing in front of open French doors. Their bodies were rather geometric and dislocated, and one had a large porthole through her chest—you could see the blue sky beyond! Two of the bodies were pink and the third was dark-brown and white skewbald. One of the pink people had a large eye running longways down one cheek. Frankie liked the background colours of greens and blues, pink and black, but she wasn't sure if she could live in the same room as those tortured human shapes.

'Picasso, dears! His Three Dancers ...'

'And what's that to remind Frankie of, pray?' demanded Frankie's mother.

'Ah—it's to show her that there's more than one way of looking at the world,' beamed Brown Aunt. 'We all need to be exposed to great art, you know, to widen our horizons—especially those of us who live in villa units!'

'Well,' muttered Frankie's father. 'Rather you than me, kid!'

Frankie gradually settled in at the high school, which she was able to walk to several streets away, and Brown Aunt did everything in her power to make Frankie feel at home. She was generally in when Frankie arrived back from school, but if not she would leave a technicolour note on the kitchen bench, usually to say she had flown off to the publishers.

Back soon ... will call at the Chinese deli en route. Get that homework out of the way so that we can run amok with the wok!

The publisher's office was close to enthralling food shops, Greek, Indian, Vietnamese, French, every sort, and Brown Aunt was a wildly adventurous cook, so

she would arrive home and draw forth the contents of
her shopping bag like a conjuror doing tricks ... out
would come water chestnuts, paper-thin fish fillets,
bunches of fennel, snow-pea shoots, crocodile steaks,
crusty garlic bread, smelly cheeses, black turtle beans.

Farm food wasn't like this, so at first Frankie was
wary of Brown Aunt's spices and stir-frys and she
longed for her Mum's roast lamb and garden spuds,
but hunger soon drove her to try these mysterious
dishes and most of them were quite edible once she'd
grown used to the new flavours. She even began to
look forward to the dramas in the kitchen as they
cooked the evening meal in a swirl of steam or blue
smoke and a barrage of chopping, sizzling, spitting
sound effects punctuated by Brown Aunt's shrieks of
triumph or dismay.

No, Frankie wasn't exactly homesick—life with
Brown Aunt was too interesting for that. She was able
to tell her mother truthfully that they didn't have
cumquat brandy for breakfast and that she had really
grown to like the Picasso in the bedroom. She would
lie in bed when she had time and look at the picture,
finding new patterns and shapes, and noticing that the
dancers seemed to move almost gracefully in spite of
their chopped-about, angular bodies.

She loved using her aunt's bathroom, which was tiled
in dusky pink and pale ivory with potted maidenhair
ferns frothing greenly on the windowsill. The thick
towels cooked gently on a heated rail and wrapped
themselves cosily round her when she stepped out of
the shower, and she loved opening the mirrored doors
of the cupboard over the vanity to feast her eyes on
the rows of exotic lotions and creams and shampoos
inside.

The farm bathroom was usually a swamp after the

boys had splashed in and out, and there were never enough hooks or rails to hang things on so that her clothes usually fell into the swamp before she'd got them safely on, and the only mirror was a tiny cracked one which her dad used for shaving, and the towels always seemed to be damp and rather threadbare.

No, she didn't miss the farm bathroom much, but she often thought of the old sink on the back verandah where they sluiced off the mud and dust and manure and dabbed their red hands dry on a grimy flour bag. This was where everyone kicked off gumboots and threw down their old hats and jackets as they came inside. On the wooden table beside the sink she could picture Mum's secateurs, Dad's oily rags, bridles and old dog collars, seed packets, buckets of overripe plums, tins of nails, a battered football, a half-empty bag of chook pellets, and old sweaters with unravelling cuffs and elbows. Pinned to the wall above were about six out-of-date calendars and an advertisement for sheep dip. When she looked at the Fred Williams picture, her mind often moved on to this picture of the farm back verandah.

What Frankie really missed was being able to fly through the back door and race for miles in any direction, towards the hills, or the woolshed, or down to the dried-up riverbed, like a bird let out of a cage. If she flew out the back door of the villa unit, she collided with the back fence after only four strides, and there wasn't much sky to be seen between the surrounding rooftops.

Mr Horace Bowley lived in Unit No.3. Old Horrie Bowley. Mrs Bowley had died two years before, and he seemed to be managing on his own, said Brown Aunt, although he kept to himself. She had given up trying to tempt him with little dishes of food, because he would look at them and then say no thanks, he had to be careful of his diet. Frankie had a feeling that Mr Bowley wouldn't understand garlic prawns or black bean sauce. Occasionally he would be sitting on his cramped front porch as she walked home from school down the driveway, and he would nod to her—but no more.

Next to him in No.2 was Mrs Cleghorn, who was even older. Brown Aunt said she was a dear old thing but you couldn't have much of a conversation with her because she agreed with absolutely everything you said. 'If I told her you had five legs and webbed feet she'd agree with me,' she told Frankie. 'It's a nightmare at Body Corporate meetings because she always wants to vote on both sides, for and against.'

'What's a Body Corporate?' gaped Frankie, imagining some fierce fat creature like a sea elephant.

'Oh, it's our little committee of management which makes rules and decisions about the units so that we can all live together in peace and harmony. That's the idea, anyway.'

'What happens when Mrs Cleghorn votes both ways?'

'In the end she always agrees to agree with Miss Limpet, because she has to live next to her.'

Miss Lydia Limpet was the terror of the units. She had lived in No.1 since it was first built and she watched the street and the gate like a trained Doberman for any signs of unacceptable behaviour. Miss Limpet had been a librarian for forty-four years, constantly on guard against unacceptable behaviour in libraries, which to her distress had become very common—people smuggling books out under their sloppy jumpers, or tearing out pages, or doodling in margins, or putting books back in the wrong place so that a book on diseases of goldfish would be lost for ages in the section on Ancient Egypt. Worst of all were those who smuggled things *in* under their jumpers, like snacks of frozen yoghurt. There was nothing more unacceptable, to Miss Limpet, than finding the pages of the Oxford Dictionary glued together with Blueberry Yog or slimy banana skins lurking behind the Encyclopaedia Britannica. Now that she'd retired she regarded everyone in the world as a potential vandal, especially Horrie Bowley, Mrs Cleghorn and Ms Shirley Brown.

When Miss Lydia Limpet heard that Frankie was coming to stay at No.4, she said sternly to Ms Brown, 'I'm not at all sure that children are allowed as residents.'

'There's no rule against it, Miss Limpet,' Brown Aunt had replied sweetly. 'After all, I have three bedrooms, so when the architect designed them he must have had several persons in mind to sleep there, including the odd child, wouldn't you say? Anyway, you can't deny the poor girl her chance of a good education—you, of all people!'

Miss Limpet had no immediate answer to that, but she watched Frankie's comings and goings like a hawk in case she dropped litter or stepped off the cement drive or loitered at the gate talking to schoolmates. Loiterers greatly lowered the tone of the units, Miss Limpet said. Frankie never felt like flying out of the front door of No.4 and running wildly up and down the drive to let off steam, because she knew the Limpet eyes would be glued to the window to observe her unruly and tone-lowering behaviour. Complaints would be made at the next Body Corporate meeting and Frankie didn't suppose that anyone would vote for *her* except her aunt.

In a Biology lesson at school one Friday the teacher announced that they were going to study Bonding. She handed each pupil in the class a day-old chicken and a small packet of chicken food and told them that they were to be responsible for their own little bird twenty-four hours a day for the weekend at least.

Most of the kids in the class had never seen a day-old chicken before and they squealed and shuddered as if they'd been asked to handle a tiger snake. But Frankie felt her spirits lift as she held the yellow fluff-ball in her cupped hands and she became bonded straight away. She was used to bonding with farm orphans, everything from lambs and baby joeys to stupid parrots who'd crash-landed out of nests before they'd learned to fly. She tucked the tiny creature inside her jumper and held it to her body to keep it warm.

'Right everybody,' the teacher sang out, 'just watch Frances. She's been a mother hen before, I'd say!'

Frankie could hardly wait to remove her chicken from the hysterical biologists and take it home to the relative peace of No.4. She walked demurely down the drive, cradling the tiny bird under her jumper and hoping the Limpet eyes were not equipped with X-ray vision. She felt a twinge of disappointment when she saw that Brown Aunt's car was out.

Horrie Bowley was sitting on his porch, staring at the pavement. Frankie decided to risk it.

'Hello Mr Bowley—look what I've got!' she said, making sure she was out of Limpet range before she held out the fluffball in her cupped hands.

Horrie Bowley's eyes and mind focused on it rather slowly, but in the end he muttered, 'Well, I'll be darned ... used to keep chooks meself. Always had chooks before *this* place. White Leghorn, is it?'

'I don't know,' said Frankie, 'but white, anyway.'

'Hen, is it?'

'I don't know that either, but I hope so—we could have fresh eggs.'

'You going to keep it then?'

'I'll have to ask my aunt, but I'd like to.'

'Well, don't let on to her in No.1,' sniffed Horrie, jerking his head towards Limpet-land. 'She'll have the Body Corporate down on you like a lorry load of wet sand, *she* will.' He thought for a moment. 'Real eggs'd be nice though. Goodonya.'

By the time Brown Aunt came in, the chicken was installed in a carton under Frankie's bed. Unfortunately Brown Aunt had brought home a large pile of chicken wings for dinner, so Frankie waited until they were hidden in the fridge before she raised the subject of fluffball. The sight of the tiny bird at first reduced the aunt to gasps of ecstasy, but then she took a firm hold on herself and began to ask stern questions such as 'Why?'

'You're studying *bonding*? But why would anyone want to bond with a chicken?'

'No—it's the other way round,' Frankie explained. 'I'm studying the chicken to see if it bonds with *me*, as it hasn't got a real mother or any other chickens to relate to, see!'

'And how long will this miraculous process take, may I ask?'

'Just a day or two. By then it should be following me round like a dog.'

'Two days! Following you round! And then what?'

Frankie looked tragic. 'Well ... unless we keep it, it will probably end up in a chicken battery.'

'*Poor thing*!' gasped Brown Aunt, in spite of herself.

51

'But Frankie darling, we can't keep it here, not in a unit! Strictly no pets allowed. Children yes, pets no. The Limpet would have us evicted.'

'It's not really a pet. It's a project, and later it would be a producer—if it's a hen.'

'You mean ... fresh eggs!' Brown Aunt's eyes glittered as she thought upon golden omelettes and puffy soufflés. 'Oh dear, well ... let's see how the weekend goes before we come to any decision, eh?'

'Mr Bowley's on our side,' said Frankie. 'He knows about chooks.'

'Does he indeed!' replied her aunt. 'Now look, if that bird is going to trail round the unit after you, I'm making you responsible for my carpets. I want to see no trace of chookpoo on the Berber, thank you.' She stroked the fluffball again. 'I'll find my hot-water bottle for you tonight, treasure,' she whispered. 'I have a distinct feeling that it is a hen,' she then announced to Frankie. 'Let's call her Lulu.'

Lulu was a smart chick. By next morning she was bonded, said Frankie.

'How do you know?' asked her aunt.

'Well, when she's out of the carton she follows me as if she's tied by an invisible thread to my foot. See?'

Frankie demonstrated and the bonded Lulu skimmed along the Berber in Frankie's wake, like a tiny yellow dinghy being towed by a container ship. 'She thinks I'm her mother.'

Over the weekend the bond grew stronger and Brown Aunt knew that to consign Lulu to a chicken battery would be an act of hideous cruelty, especially after the little bird had been introduced to the luxury of Berber carpets underfoot and a hottie in bed at night.

The Biology class had been given the choice of handing back their chickens on Monday morning or of taking complete responsibility for them at home, for ever. Frankie felt fairly sure that Brown Aunt would be a pushover. She'd already been getting up during the night to refill the hottie for Lulu, and she called her 'fluffpot' and 'chickabid' and other mushy names. But on Sunday, Frankie had to make sure. 'Can I keep her?' she asked.

Brown Aunt endeavoured to look stern. 'You know the rules, Frankie—no pets. It's all very well while Lulu is a fluffball, but she can't live under your bed for long. There is already a strong whiff of the farm-yard in there.'

'Yes, it makes me feel at home,' said Frankie. 'I like it.'

'But when she gets bigger she'll have to go outside, and then the Limpet will find out and that will be that.'

'Mr Bowley doesn't mind. We just need to get Mrs Cleghorn to vote for Lulu and that will be three to one against Limpet. Anyway, what difference would it make to *her*? She wouldn't even see Lulu from her place!'

To prove her point, Frankie took Lulu on to the lawn behind No.4 and the chicken scooted about, cheeping. Frankie scattered some crushed wheat and made motherly clucking noises until Lulu began to peck and scratch in the grass. Horrie Bowley peered round the back corner near his clothes line.

'Are you keeping it?' he hissed.

'I hope so,' Frankie hissed back. 'You don't mind, do you?'

'No fear. I'll build a chook house for it if you like. I can salvage some bits of two-by-four from that building site up the street—there's a heap of rubbish out the front and they wouldn't mind.' Horrie had never looked so animated in Frankie's memory.

Brown Aunt gave in, of course. She even conspired with Horrie Bowley to smuggle lengths of two-by-four down to the back unit in the boot of her car when Miss Limpet was at the bank. Miss Limpet's banking and shopping routines were so rigidly regular that it was easy to know when smuggling could be safely carried out. Horrie and Ms Brown interviewed the supervisor at the building site, who personally selected superior pieces of timber off-cuts from his rubbish pile and told them to take anything else they needed. He even gave Horrie a handful of galvanised nails for the job. 'We had chooks when I was a kid,' he explained. 'I really miss 'em.'

By the time Miss Limpet had returned from the bank, the timber had been neatly stacked behind No.4, out of sight, and Horrie Bowley, too, was out of sight in his kitchen drawing up architectural plans for a chook house on the back of an envelope.

'There's a Body Corporate meeting on Thursday evening,' said Brown Aunt that night as she grated a mound of mozzarella cheese ready for a sumptuous homemade pizza. Frankie was chopping scarlet capsicum and mushrooms. 'I'll have to raise the matter of Lulu.'

Frankie stopped chopping. 'Do you *have* to?'

'Yes darling, I do—there's no point in Horrie building a chook house unless we're allowed to keep her.'

'But the Limpet will go into orbit!'

'That's nothing new. I'll just have to be very persuasive—and somehow we'll have to keep Mrs Cleghorn on side.'

'Cleghorn rhymes with Leghorn,' mused Frankie. 'That might help.'

'Ha!' laughed her aunt. 'Do you suppose that's an omen?'

The matter of Lulu came under Any Other Business on the agenda. The Body Corporate was managed by young Mr Scales from a legal firm. He was terrified of Miss Limpet, who was a stickler for correct procedure and always called him 'Mr Chair'. However, this meeting had proceeded smoothly right to the end and Mr Scales was looking forward to escaping in time to see the late movie as he shuffled his papers together and asked, 'Any other business?'

Ms Shirley Brown said firmly, 'Yes, there is,' and Mr Scales suppressed a groan and listened with growing dismay as she explained about Lulu and Frankie. Mr Scales knew, everybody knew, that many a Body Corporate had come to grief over the twin problems of pets and children, especially when there was a dragon like Miss Lydia Limpet on the committee.

Miss Limpet was even now coming to the boil. 'Absolutely *NOT*!' she cried, quite forgetting to address her remarks to Mr Chair. 'Strictly no pets allowed, as you very well know, Miss Brown!'

'No, indeed,' echoed Mrs Cleghorn.

Ms Shirley Brown squared her jaw. 'I must make it clear that Lulu is not exactly a pet. She is a working hen—or she soon will be.'

'That's right,' agreed Mrs Cleghorn.

Mr Scales in the Chair was out of his depth.

'She'll be a layer—an egg-producer,' explained Ms Brown.

'Manure, too,' contributed Horrie Bowley.

This was a word that rarely passed the lips of Miss

Limpet, but now she found herself screeching it aloud. '*Manure*!! We can't have *that ... substance* lying around, polluting the very air we breathe!'

'Rubbish!' snorted Ms Brown. 'We could invest in a compost bin—and what with our kitchen scraps and lawn clippings and Lulu's manure and some worms, we'd have the best pansies and tomatoes in the street.' She had just been proofreading a booklet on organic gardening which was the source of this sudden inspiration.

'How lovely!' beamed Mrs Cleghorn. 'Pansies are my favourites!'

'Lovely? *Lovely*!' glared Miss Limpet. 'Next thing we'll all be getting psittacosis!'

'So we will,' gasped Mrs Cleghorn, wondering if it was a new type of shrub.

'No you *won't*—psittacosis is parrot's disease!' snapped Ms Brown. 'Lulu is not a parrot—she's a hen!'

'Ladies, ladies,' pleaded Mr Scales from the Chair, wishing he had a gavel to thump on the table. 'Let us keep calm. There is a regulation which prohibits the keeping of pets in these units, certainly, but there is also a clause which states ... *except by a majority agreement*. This means we can vote on it. Has anyone anything to add to the discussion before we do so?'

Horrie Bowley cleared his throat. 'Well, I like chooks, see, and I'd be pleased to build a chook house down the back there.' He didn't mention the waiting pile of two-by-fours or the working drawings or the fact that he had spent a whole evening sharpening his saw. '*You* won't even be able to see it down there,' he glared at Miss Limpet, 'so I dunno what you're belly-aching about.'

Miss Lydia Limpet had the breath knocked out of

her momentarily. Horrie Bowley had never spoken up like that before, but it only confirmed what she had always suspected—that he was coarse, using words like 'belly-aching' and 'manure' in that company.

Ms Brown seized the chance of Miss Limpet's breathlessness to sum up, stressing the point that her niece Frances had come to the city to further her education, but she was still a country girl at heart, missing her family and the farm. 'This little hen has come into her life at a crucial moment and it would be heartless of us not to let her keep it,' she appealed. Visions of cheesey omelettes and golden soufflés also swam through her mind but she carefully kept these to herself.

'Poor little girl—why shouldn't she keep Lulu then?' purred Mrs Cleghorn.

'I've just *told* you,' snapped Lydia Limpet. 'Filth and disease. And besides, that fowl will be the thin edge of the wedge. Next thing *you*, Mrs Cleghorn, will be wanting to keep a German Shepherd dog.'

'Ooh, I will not!' answered Mrs Cleghorn, whose secret ambition was a racing greyhound.

Brown Aunt told Frankie later that this was the first time she had ever heard Mrs Cleghorn disagree with anybody, let alone Miss Limpet. 'And I must hand it to Mr Scales,' she said, 'he seized the moment and put it to the vote there and then and it was three to one in favour!'

'Didn't Mrs Cleghorn try to vote against, too?'

'Oh, of course, but she wavered and Mr Scales told her that she couldn't vote twice, so there you are darling—Lulu can stay and the Limpet can like it or lump it!'

Frankie and her aunt engaged in a long bear hug and then they filled Lulu's hottie for the night.

Next day Horrie brought in his working plans for approval. Lulu's residence would be set against the fence, which was to be its back wall. It had a roof sloping to the front and chicken wire on the other three sides. Horrie had designed a nest box sticking out at one end, and by lifting a hinged lid you could look inside to find any eggs. At the other end of the chook house was a wire covered door, big enough for Frankie to squeeze through when the cage needed mucking out. There was a perch for Lulu to sleep on, sheltered by the fence. It was a very plain house, but much better than a battery, and Horrie said that Lulu could come out for exercise on the grass sometimes. Frankie would be able to see Lulu's house from her bedroom window.

As the chook house began to grow, so did Lulu. Her neat little feet and yellow legs grew long and rangy. Unfurling quills and feathers blotched her charming fluff, and she hopped about flapping her silly wings. Her soft little beak became hard and flinty. The black twirls of chookpoo on the Berber were daily larger and more difficult to remove, and the farmyard smell intensified. Brown Aunt watched Horrie's progress with impatience. She could almost find herself agreeing with Miss Limpet about the polluting tendencies of manure, but she didn't complain to Frankie. After all, she had backed Frankie in this poultry farming venture, and she couldn't desert her now.

At last the day arrived for Lulu to move into her new apartment. Frankie filled a new water dish and a tin full of grain for the chook house, and threw in some lettuce leaves before carrying Lulu out and pushing her through the door. Horrie Bowley and Brown Aunt joined the ceremonial party. Horrie was proud beyond measure of his chook house, Brown Aunt was immensely relieved about her carpet and could now concentrate on dreams of future omelettes, while Frankie sank to her knees to watch Lulu explore her new home. After some time, Frankie said:

'I don't think she understands about the perch.'

'Well, you're her mother, darling,' said Brown Aunt. 'Show her how it's done.'

Frankie reached through the doorway, grabbed Lulu and balanced her on the perch. Lulu swayed and wobbled a bit, until she'd learnt how to grip, and then she began flapping her wings and stretching and sidling to and fro along the perch. Lulu was a quick learner.

Each morning when Frankie climbed out of bed, she went first to the window to check on Lulu, and the little bird would be sidling along the front of the cage, waiting for Frankie to bring her breakfast. After school, Lulu would be allowed out to exercise on the lawn, and on Saturdays Frankie would clean out the bottom of the cage and put all the mess into the new green compost bin which Brown Aunt and Horrie had bought between them. Brown Aunt had smuggled it home in the boot of her car when Miss Limpet was at the bank. Horrie was already planning a new garden bed for pansies and Brown Aunt had decided to dig up a corner of her back lawn and go in for a few exotic vegetables.

Lulu kept growing. Then, one day, it was time for Frankie to go home for the holidays. She was torn in half—wanting to go and see her family and the farm, and not wanting to leave Lulu.

'Don't be silly, darling,' said Brown Aunt. 'Horrie has offered to care for Lulu, and he's dying to do it too, so don't *worry*. And I'll keep an eagle eye on her as well.'

Horrie spent half his days caring for Lulu. He even began to plan some improvements to the chook house. Brown Aunt took the opportunity to have the Berber steam cleaned and fumigated while Frankie was away.

Then, one morning, while Shirley Brown was pottering about preparing breakfast, there was a spinechilling noise from the back garden. A strangled cry—Lulu was in trouble! There it was again! Predators! A dog? A chicken thief? A giant rat? Brown Aunt dropped her croissant and ran to the back door. At the same moment Horrie Bowley peered round the corner, his face half lathered in shaving soap.

'What was it?' cried Brown Aunt. 'I'll never forgive myself if something's befallen that hen!'

'I dunno ...' gasped Horrie. 'She *looks* all right.'

They stared at Lulu, who was standing on her perch looking quite normal. No dogs, rats, chicken thieves in sight. But then ... Lulu stretched up on her legs, arched her neck and emitted another fearful cry.

'Is she choking?' whispered Brown Aunt.

Horrie was appalled. 'Crikey! Ah, no ... not choking I wouldn't say.' He glanced sideways at Ms Brown, nervously. 'Not really choking ... more like, um ... crowing.'

'Crowing? *CROWING*? Do you mean ... you *don't* mean ...?'

'Well, um ... yairs, that's right. Look's as though she's not really a hen after all. More like a rooster. Mind you, it's often very hard to tell the difference when they're youngsters—but I *was* beginning to wonder about her ... its big feet, and its comb was getting on the biggish side, too. Pity, really.'

'A pity? It's a *disaster*! We can't have a rooster crowing here—that Limpet woman will really have some-

thing to complain about, and we're all going to look
like idiots. And those eggs, what about those eggs?
And what are we going to tell Frankie?' Lulu shrieked
again. 'My heaven, we'll have to do something quickly, before Miss Limpet hears it!'

'Just a tick.' Horrie vanished and returned with a
large grey blanket which he draped over the chook
house. 'There, sh ... he'll think it's night-time and
he'll shut up for a while. It'll give us time to work
something out.'

'Come inside—we need black coffee,' moaned
Brown Aunt, ushering Horrie into her kitchen. His
face was still lathery, so she offered him a towel. 'You
know, it's largely my fault,' she said. 'I felt convinced
it was a hen and I called it Lulu, that very first day. It
was just wishful thinking about the fresh eggs. I was
too greedy.'

'I could chop its head off,' mumbled Horrie Bowley
from inside the towel.

Brown Aunt stared at him. 'I didn't hear that,' she
said sternly. 'There's to be no blood spilled on *my* back
lawn. No—we'll have to trade him in on a real hen.'

'You won't get much for him—nobody wants roosters.'

'I don't care—I'll just have to pay the difference.'

As soon as Miss Limpet had set out for the shops that
morning, Brown Aunt and Horrie Bowley bundled
Lulu into a carton and headed for a livestock market
in a distant outer suburb.

That evening, Brown Aunt rang Frankie at the
farm.

'Darling ... it's about Lulu ...'

'What's happened? Is she ...? I know, she's dead ... is
that it?'

'No, no, no! She's perfectly well, but ... um ... she's no longer with us.'

'What do you mean—has she escaped?'

'Of course not. She ... um ... well, she's had a sex change. You know, she began to crow.'

As Frankie relayed this news to her family, there was an explosion of background laughter and Frankie's father muttered, 'I said it would do Shirley good to live with a kid for a while. She's discovering the facts of life!'

'Don't be silly, aunt,' snorted Frankie into the phone. 'Lulu didn't have a sex change—only in your mind. She must have been a rooster all along!'

'Well yes, of course she was—but you see, Frankie darling, we couldn't have her ... *him* here crowing his head off, because of the neighbours—especially the Limpet. So I made an executive decision. And I'm terribly sorry about the bonding.'

'What have you done—you haven't chopped his head off have you?'

'How could you think that, after all those hotties I filled for him in the dead of night? No, the good news is that Horrie and I found this *lovely* poultry man called Stavros at a market, and ... wait for it ... we've traded Lulu in for two laying pullets!'

'Two!' exclaimed Frankie. 'Laying!'

'Yes, Stavros convinced me that it was false economy to have just one—and I'm sure they'll lay better if they have competition.'

'You mean they'll egg each other on!' giggled Frankie. She couldn't help laughing at Brown Aunt, but at the same time a tear oozed down her cheek as she felt her Lulu-bond being wrenched apart.

'Oooh, just wait until you see them darling, they are gorgeous, white with black speckled necks—Light

Sussex they're called! You can give them names when you get back next week, and by that time, we could be up to our first omelette!'

Frankie wiped her cheek on her sleeve.

'Oh, and one last thing darling—this you'll never believe. Today Mrs Cleghorn saw Miss Limpet slip into the pet shop down by the bank, so Mrs C. followed her in.'

'What was she doing?' asked Frankie.

'She was pricing budgies!'

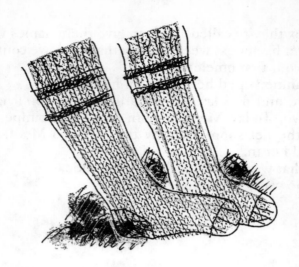

Aunt Millicent

'I,' said Angelica Tonks, grandly, 'have eight uncles and eleven aunts.' Angelica Tonks had more of most things than anyone else. She held the class record for pairs of fashion sneakers and Derwent pencil sets, and her pocket-money supply was endless. Now, it seemed, she also had the largest uncle-and-aunt collection in town. Her classmates squirmed and made faces at each other. *Awful* Angelica Tonks.

Mr Wilfred Starling dusted the chalk from his bony hands and sighed. 'Well, Angelica, aren't you a lucky one to have nineteen uncles and aunts. You'll just have to choose the most interesting one to write about, won't you?'

'But they're *all* interesting,' objected Angelica.

'The Tonks family is a wonderfully interesting family, you know. It will be terribly hard to choose just one.'

There were more squirms. The class was fed up with the wonderfully interesting Tonks family. In fact, Mr Wilfred Starling nearly screamed. He just managed to swallow his exasperation, which sank down to form a hard bubble in his stomach. Straightening his thin shoulders, he said, 'Right, everyone, copy down this week's homework assignment from the board. And remember, Angelica, a pen-portrait of just *one* aunt or uncle is all I want. Just *one*.' *Please not a whole gallery of tedious and terrible Tonkses*, he thought to himself.

The class began to write. Jamie Nutbeam, sitting behind Angelica, leaned forward and hissed, 'If the rest of your family is so *wonderfully interesting*, they must be a big improvement on you, Honky! And, any-way, I bet the aunt I write about will beat any of yours!'

'I bet she won't,' Angelica hissed back. 'She'll be so *boring*. What's her name, this boring aunt?'

Jamie finished copying and put down his pen. 'Aunt Millicent, and she's pretty special.'

'Millicent!' scoffed Angelica. 'What a name! No-one's called Millicent these days!'

'*QUIET*, you two!' barked Mr Starling, massaging his stomach, 'and start tidying up, everyone—it's time for the bell.' *Oh bliss*, he thought.

As the classroom emptied, Jamie lingered behind.

'What is it, Jamie?' asked Mr Starling wearily, piling his books and papers together and trying not to burp.

'Well, the trouble is I haven't any aunts or uncles to do a portrait of,' said Jamie, turning rather red, 'so is it all right if I make one up? An aunt?'

'Oh, I see! Well, in that case ... yes, perfectly all right,' replied Mr Starling. He gazed rather sadly out the window. 'The most interesting characters in the world are usually the made-up ones, you know, Jamie. Think of Sherlock Holmes and Alice and Dr Who and Indiana Jones ...'

Jamie interrupted. 'Does anyone need to know I've made her up? This aunt?'

'Well, *I* won't say anything,' promised Mr Starling. 'It's for you to make her seem real so we all believe in her. You go home and see what you can dream up.'

'She has a name already,' Jamie called back as he left the room. 'She's Aunt Millicent.'

Aunt Millicent Nutbeam! The hard bubble in Mr Starling's stomach began to melt away.

That evening, Jamie Nutbeam said to his family at large, 'Did you know that awful Angelica Tonks has eight uncles and eleven aunts?'

'Well, everybody knows that they're a big family,' replied his mother.

'Prolific, I'd call it,' grunted Jamie's father from behind his newspaper.

'Yes, dear—prolific. Now, Mrs Tonks was a Miss Blizzard,' continued Mrs Nutbeam, 'and there are lots of Blizzards around here as well as Tonkses, all related, no doubt. But fancy nineteen! Who told you there were nineteen, Jamie?'

'She did—old Honky Tonks herself. She told the whole class *and* Mr Starling—boasting away as usual. She's a *pill*.' Jamie was jotting things on paper as he talked. 'We have to write a pen-portrait of an aunt or uncle for homework, and Honky can't decide which one to do because they're all so *wonderfully interesting*, she says. Urk!' He paused and then added, 'I'm doing Aunt Millicent.'

Jamie's father peered over the top of his newspaper. 'Aunt who?'

'Who's Aunt Millicent?' demanded Jamie's sister, Nerissa.

'You haven't got an Aunt Millicent,' said his mother. 'You haven't any aunts at all, *or* uncles, for that matter.'

'I *know* I haven't,' Jamie snapped. 'It's *hopeless* belonging to a nuclear family! It's unfair—I mean, awful Honky has nineteen aunts and uncles and Nerissa and I haven't got any, not one.' Jamie ground the pencil between his teeth.

'You won't have any teeth either, if you munch pencils like that,' remarked his father, who was a dentist.

Jamie glowered, spitting out wet splinters.

'Anyway, he's right,' announced Nerissa. 'It would be great to have even one aunt or uncle. Then we might have some cousins, too. Everyone else has cousins. Angelica Tonks probably has about a hundred-and-twenty-seven.'

'Well, I'm sorry,' sighed Mrs Nutbeam, 'but your father and I are both "onlys" and there's nothing we can do about that, is there? Not a thing! Now, what's all this about an Aunt Millicent?'

'Oh, it's okay,' grumbled her son. 'Mr Starling said to write about *an* aunt or uncle, not exactly *my* aunt or uncle. He says I can invent one.'

'Will you explain that she's not real?' asked Nerissa, doubtfully.

'Mr Starling says I don't have to, and he's not going to tell. He says I have to make people believe that she *is* real. Anyway, I don't want Honky Tonks to know that she's made up, because Aunt Millicent is going to be amazing—much better than any of those boring Tonkses. It's time Honky was taken down a peg or two.'

Dr Nutbeam quite understood how Jamie felt.

From time to time Angelica Tonks visited his dentist's chair. She would brag about her 'perfect' teeth if there was nothing to be fixed, but if she needed a filling her shrieks of 'agony' would upset everyone in the waiting room and Mrs Tonks would call Dr Nutbeam a *brute*. He was often tempted to give Angelica a general anaesthetic and post her home in a large jiffy bag.

Now he folded his newspaper; Jamie's project sounded rather fun. 'Right, Jamie,' he said, 'tell us about Aunt Millicent and let us get some facts straight. Is she my sister, or Mum's? We must get that settled to start with.'

'I can't decide,' frowned Jamie. 'What do you think?'

'She'd better be your sister, dear,' said Mrs Nutbeam calmly to her husband. 'I grew up here and everyone knows I was an only child, but you came from another town. You're more mysterious.'

Dr Nutbeam looked pleased. 'Mm ... mm. That's nice ... having a sister, I mean. Is she younger than me?'

'No, older,' said Jamie.

'Where does she live?' asked Nerissa. 'Has she a family of her own? Lots of cousins for us?'

'No way—she hasn't time for all that sort of thing. And she doesn't live anywhere in particular.'

Mrs Nutbeam looked puzzled. 'What *do* you mean, dear? What does Auntie Millicent do, exactly?'

'She's an explorer,' said Jamie, proudly. 'She works for foreign governments, and she's terribly busy—flat out.'

There was something of a pause. Then Dr Nutbeam said, 'Ah,' and stroked his bald patch. 'That explains why we haven't seen her for so long.'

'What does she explore?' demanded Nerissa. 'Is there anything left in the world to look for?'

Jamie was beginning to feel a bit rushed. 'Well, I'm not sure yet, but foreign governments need people like her to search for water in deserts and rich mineral deposits and endangered species and things ... you know.'

Nerissa lay on the floor with her eyes closed and began to imagine her new aunt slashing a path through tangled jungle vines, searching for a rare species of dark blue frog. The mosquitoes were savage. The leeches were huge and bloated. Aunt Millicent's machete was razor sharp ...

'This is all very unexpected,' murmured Mrs Nutbeam, 'to have a sister-in-law who is an explorer, I mean. I wonder how you get started in that sort of career?' Her own job as an assistant in an antique and curio shop suddenly seemed rather drab.

Dr Nutbeam was staring at the wall. In his mind's eye he clearly saw his sister on a swaying rope suspension bridge above a terrifying ravine. She was leading a band of native bearers to the other side. How much more adventurous, he thought, than drilling little holes in people's teeth. He wrenched his gaze back to Jamie and asked, 'Do we know what Millie is actually exploring at present?'

Jamie munched his pencil for a moment and then said, 'She's in Africa, somewhere near the middle, but I'm not sure where, exactly.'

'In the middle of Africa, is she?' echoed Dr Nutbeam. 'Mm ... then it wouldn't surprise me if she were in the Cameroons. There's a lot of dense forest in the Cameroons, you know.'

'I thought Cameroons were things to eat,' frowned Nerissa. 'Sort of coconut biscuits.'

'No, no, dear, those are macaroons,' said her mother.

'*They're* bad for your teeth, too,' remarked her father, absently, 'like eating pencils.'

Jamie fetched the atlas and found a map of Africa. His father stood behind him, peering at it. 'There it is, in the middle on the left-hand side, just under the bump.'

'It's called Cameroon here,' Jamie said. 'Just one of them.'

'Well, in my day there was East Cameroon and West Cameroon, see,' pointed his father, 'and sometimes we lumped them together and called them Cameroons. Look—here's the equator just to the south, so it must be pretty hot and steamy at sea-level.'

'Poor Millicent,' sighed Mrs Nutbeam. 'I do hope her feet don't swell in the heat, with all that walking.'

Jamie examined the map closely. 'That's peculiar— the north border of the Cameroons seems to be floating in a big lake ... um, Lake Chad ... it looks all swampy, with funny dotted lines and things. I bet that bit needs exploring. They've probably lost their border in the mud and Aunt Millicent could be on an expedition to find it.'

'Is she all by herself?' asked Nerissa. 'I'd be scared in a place like that.'

'Of course she's not by herself,' snorted Jamie. 'She works for a foreign government, don't forget, and she'd have a whole support team of porters and cooks and scientists and things.'

'She must be an expert at something herself, don't you think?' suggested Mrs Nutbeam. 'I would imagine that she's a surveyor.'

'Yes, she'd use one of those instruments you look through, on legs,' added Nerissa.

'You mean a theodolite, dimwit,' answered her brother.

'She'd certainly need one of those, if she's measuring angles and distances and drawing maps,' agreed Dr Nutbeam. 'My word, what a clever old sister I have!'

'I wonder if she was good at Geography at school?' said Nerissa.

'Well, you'll be able to ask Grandma tomorrow. She's coming for her winter visit, remember?'

'Oh help! What'll Grandma *say*?' gasped Jamie. 'Do you think she'll mind? I mean—we've invented a daughter for her without asking!'

'I shouldn't think she'd mind,' said his mother. 'We'll break the news to her carefully and see how she takes it.'

Grandma Nutbeam, as it turned out, was delighted.

'How exciting!' she exclaimed. 'I always wanted a daughter, and it's been very lonely since Grandpa died. Now I'll have a new interest! Just show me on the map where Millicent is at the moment, please dear.'

Jamie pointed to the dotted lines in swampy Lake Chad near the top end of the Cameroons, and Grandma stared in astonishment.

'Gracious heaven! What an extraordinary place to go to, the silly girl! I hope she's remembered her quinine tablets. Millicent was never very good at looking after herself, you know. Let me see—I think I'll get some wool tomorrow and knit her some good stout hiking socks.'

Jamie blinked. 'There's no need to do that, Grandma. She's not really real, you know.'

'Well, she'll be more real to me if I make her some socks,' Grandma declared.

'Wouldn't they be rather hot in the Cameroons?' objected Nerissa. 'It's awfully near the equator, don't forget.'

'Woollen socks are best in any climate,' said Grandma firmly. 'They breathe.'

'Now, Mother,' interrupted Dr Nutbeam, 'you can tell us what Millicent was like as a girl. I can't remember her very well, as she was so much older than me, but I have a feeling that she ran away from home a lot.'

Grandma pondered a moment. 'Now that you mention it, she did. She did indeed. I thought we'd have to chain her up sometimes! We lived near the edge of town, you'll remember, and Millie would look out towards the paddocks and hills and say that she wanted to know what was over the horizon, or where the birds were flying to, or where the clouds came from behind the hills. We never knew where she'd be off to next—but she certainly ended up in the right job! I'm so glad she became an explorer. If I were a bit younger and had better feet, I might even go and join her. It would be most interesting to see the Cameroons. It's full of monkeys, I believe.'

'Was Aunt Millicent good at Geography at school?' Nerissa remembered to ask.

'Let me think—yes, she must have been because one year she won a prize for it, and the prize was a book called *Lives of the Great Explorers*.'

'Well, there you are,' remarked Mrs Nutbeam. 'That's probably how it all started.'

Next day, Grandma Nutbeam began to knit a pair of explorer's socks. She decided on khaki with dark blue stripes round the top.

Angelica Tonks had found it so difficult to select one of the nineteen aunts and uncles, that her pen-portrait was left until the very last minute and then scrawled out in a great hurry. She had finally chosen Aunt Daisy Blizzard, Mrs Tonks's eldest sister.

Mr Wilfred Starling asked Angelica to read her portrait to the class first, to get it over with. As he had

72

expected and as Jamie Nutbeam had hoped, Angelica's aunt sounded anything but wonderfully interesting. She had always lived in the same street, her favourite colour was deep purple and she grew African violets on the bathroom shelf, but that was about all.

Many of the other portraits weren't much better, although there was one uncle who had fallen into Lake Burley Griffin and been rescued by a passing Member of Parliament. Someone else's aunt had competed in a penny-farthing bicycle race in northern Tasmania, only to capsize and sprain both her knees; and there was a great-uncle who had been present at the opening of the Sydney Harbour Bridge in 1932, but couldn't remember it at all as he'd been asleep in his pram at the time.

Mr Starling saved Jamie's portrait until last, hoping for the best. Jamie cleared his throat nervously and began:

'I have never met Aunt Millicent and no-one in my family knows her very well, as she hasn't been in Australia for a long time. This is because Aunt Millicent is an explorer ...'

Mr Wilfred Starling had been hoping for a bright spot in his day, and it looked as if Aunt Millicent Nutbeam would be it. He smiled happily when Jamie explained how Millicent had gained her early training as an explorer by regularly running away from home. He sighed with pleasure as Jamie described the swampy region of Lake Chad, where Millicent was searching through the mud and papyrus for the northern border of the Cameroons. He positively beamed when he heard that Grandma Nutbeam was knitting explorer's socks for her daughter.

The rest of the class sat spellbound as Jamie read on, except for Angelica Tonks, whose scowl grew darker by the minute. Jamie had barely finished his portrait when her hand was waving furiously.

Mr Starling's beam faded. 'What *is* it, Angelica?'

'I don't believe it. Women don't go exploring! I think Jamie's made it all up! He's a cheat!'

Mr Starling's stomach lurched, but before he had time to say anything the other girls in the class rose up in a passion and rounded on Angelica.

'Who *says* women don't go exploring?'

'Women can do anything they want to these days, Angelica Tonks! Don't you know that?'

'*I'd* really like to be an explorer or something—maybe a test pilot.'

'Well, *I'd* like to be a diver and explore the ocean floor and have a good look at the *Titanic*.'

'What does your aunt wear when she's at work?'

'What colour are her new socks?'

The boys began to join in.

'Can your aunt really use a machete?'

'How many languages can she speak?'

'Does she always carry a gun? I bet she's a crack shot!'

'How does a theodolite work?'

The clamour was so great that hardly anyone heard the bell. Angelica Tonks heard it and vanished in a sulk. Mr Starling heard it and happily gathered up his books. He gave Jamie a secret wink as he left the room.

The end of the assignment was not the end of Aunt Millicent. At school, the careers teacher ran some special sessions on 'Challenging Occupations for Women' after he had been stormed by the girls from Jamie's class for information about becoming test pilots, mobile-crane drivers, buffalo hunters and ocean-floor mappers. The science teacher was asked to explain the workings of a theodolite to the class.

At home, Aunt Millicent settled happily into the Nutbeam family, who all followed her adventures with great interest. Dr Nutbeam brought home library books about the Cameroons and Central Africa. Jamie roared his way through one called *The Bafut Beagles*. Mrs Nutbeam rummaged through an old storeroom at the curio shop and began to collect exotic objects. She brought home a brace of hunting spears from Kenya, which she hung on the family room wall.

'Just the sort of souvenir Millicent could have sent us,' she explained. 'See—those marks on the blades are very probably dried bloodstains.'

Another time she unwrapped a stuffed mongoose, announcing that Auntie had sent this from India on one of her earlier trips.

Jamie and Nerissa stroked it. 'What a funny animal,' said Nerissa. 'Like a weasel.'

Grandma was knitting her way down the second sock leg. 'That funny animal is a very brave creature,' she admonished, tapping the mongoose with her knitting needle. 'I'll always remember Kipling's story of Rikki-Tikki-Tavi and how he fought that dreadful king cobra. Brrr!'

'Who won?' asked Jamie.

'You could read it yourself and find out, young man,' said Grandma, starting to knit a new row. 'I expect Millicent has met a few cobras in her time.'

Nerissa had splendid dreams nearly every night. Aunt Millicent strode through most of them, wielding her machete or shouldering her theodolite. Sometimes Nerissa found herself wading through swirling rivers or swinging on jungle vines like a gibbon. Jamie was often there, too, or some of her school friends, or Grandma followed by a mongoose on a lead. Once, Mrs Nutbeam speared a giant toad, which exploded and woke Nerissa

75

up. In another dream, Nerissa's father was polishing the fangs of a grinning crocodile, which lay back in the dentist's chair with its long tail tucked neatly under the steriliser. It looked slightly like Mrs Tonks.

Mrs Nutbeam brought home still more curios: a bamboo flute and a small tom-tom which Jamie and Nerissa soon learnt to play. Mysterious drumbeats and thin flutey tunes drifted along the street from the Nutbeams' house. School friends came to beat the tom-tom and to stroke the mongoose and to see how the explorer's socks were growing.

'Will you be sending them off soon, to the Cameroons?' they asked Grandma, who was turning the heel of the second sock.

'I think I'll make another pair, perhaps even three pairs,' replied Grandma. 'I might just as well send a large parcel as a small one.'

'Yes, and then Aunt Millie will have spare pairs of socks she can wash,' said Nerissa. 'Socks must get very smelly near the equator.'

Word of Millicent Nutbeam, intrepid explorer, began to spread through the town. Children told their families about the spears, the tom-tom, the mongoose and the khaki socks. Not every small town could claim to be connected to a famous international explorer—it was exciting news.

Angelica Tonks, however, told her mother that she didn't believe Jamie's aunt was an explorer at all. 'I bet he just invented that to make his aunt seem more interesting than all the rest,' she scoffed.

Mrs Tonks sniffed a good deal and then decided it was time to have a dental checkup. 'I'll get to the bottom of that Millicent Nutbeam, you mark my words,' she told Angelica, as she telephoned Dr Nutbeam's surgery for an appointment.

'Well, well—good morning Mrs Tonks,' said Dr Nutbeam, a few days later. 'We haven't seen you for a while! Just lie right back in the chair please, and relax!'

Mrs Tonks lay back, but she didn't relax one bit. Her eyes were sharp and suspicious. 'Good morning, Dr Nutbeam. How is the family?' she enquired. 'And how is your sister?'

Dr Nutbeam pulled on his rubber gloves. 'My sister? Which one? ... Er, probe, please nurse.'

Before he could say 'Open wide', Mrs Tonks snapped, 'Your sister the so-called explorer. Huh! The one in the Cameroons.'

'Ah, *that* sister. You mean Millicent ... now, just open wider and turn this way a little. Yes, our Millie, she does work so hard ... oops, there's a beaut cavity! A real crater!' He crammed six plugs of cotton wool around Mrs Tonks's gums. 'My word, what a lot of saliva! We'll have some suction please nurse, and just wipe that dribble from the patient's chin.' He continued to poke and scrape Mrs Tonks's molars, none too gently. 'Ah, here's another trouble spot. Mm ... have you ever been to the Cameroons, Mrs Tonks?'

Mrs Tonks's eyes glared. She tried to shake her head, but could only gurgle, 'Arggg ...'

'No, I didn't think you had. Such a fascinating place!' Dr Nutbeam turned on the squealing high-speed drill and bored into her decaying tooth, spraying water all over her chin.

When he had told his family about this encounter with Mrs Tonks, his wife complained, 'It's all very well for you. *You* can just cram people's mouths full of wadding and metal contraptions and suction tubes if they start asking awkward questions, but what am I supposed to do?'

The truth was that increasing numbers of townsfolk were calling at the antique shop where Mrs Nutbeam worked. They were eager to know more about Millicent Nutbeam and her adventurous life. They felt proud of her.

'It's getting quite tricky,' Mrs Nutbeam explained. 'People are asking to see photos of Millicent and wanting us to talk at the elderly citizens' club about her. This aunt is becoming an embarrassment. I wish people weren't so curious. Sometimes I don't know what to say!'

Grandma found herself on slippery ground, too, when she met the postman at the gate.

'Morning,' he said, sorting through his mailbag. 'You must be Jamie's grandmother, then.'

'Yes, I am,' Grandma replied, rather surprised.

'Mother of the explorer, eh?'

'Gracious!' exclaimed Grandma. 'Fancy you knowing about that!'

'Oh, my girl Julie has told us all about it. She's in Jamie's class at school. Funny thing—Julie's gone round the twist since she heard about all that exploring business. Says she wants to buy a camel and ride it round Australia, and one of her friends is going to apply for a job on an oil rig. I ask you!'

'Well, that's nice,' said Grandma, soothingly. 'Girls are so enterprising these days.'

'Huh! Mad, I call it.' The postman held out a bundle of letters. 'Here you are. Now, that's *another* funny thing—the Nutbeams don't get much foreign mail, come to think of it. You'd think the explorer would write to them more often, her being in the travelling line.'

Grandma breathed deeply. 'Oh, it's not easy, you know, writing letters when you're exploring. For one

78

thing, there's never a decent light in the tent at night—and besides, there's hardly ever a post office to hand when you need it.' She glanced through the letters. 'Goodness! There's one from South America ... Peru!'

'That's what made me wonder. Is it from her?' asked the postman, eagerly.

'Her? Ah ... Millicent. I don't know. It's for Dr Nutbeam, my son, and it's typed. Anyway, as far as we know, Millicent is still in the Cameroons, although we've not had word for some time.'

'She could have moved on, couldn't she?' suggested the postman. 'Peru, eh? Oh well, I'd better move on, too. G'day to you!'

At school, Julie the postman's daughter said to Jamie, 'Why has your auntie gone to South America? What's she exploring now?'

'Who said she's gone to South America?' demanded Jamie. He felt he was losing control of Aunt Millicent.

'My dad said there was a letter from her in Peru,' replied Julie.

'Well, no-one told *me*,' growled Jamie.

At home he announced, 'Julie is telling everybody that our Aunt Millicent is in Peru! What's she talking about? What's happening?'

Grandma stopped knitting. 'Julie. Is that the name of the postman's girl?'

'Yes—her dad said there was a letter for us from Auntie in Peru, or somewhere mad.'

'Oh, I remember—he asked me about it,' said Grandma.

'Well ... what did you *say*?' wailed Jamie.

'I just said I didn't know who the letter was from and that I thought Millicent was still in the

Cameroons, but that we hadn't heard for a while where she was. That's all.'

'The letter from Peru,' chuckled Dr Nutbeam, 'is about the World Dental Conference on plaque, which is being held next year in Lima. It has nothing to do with Millicent.'

'Well of *course* it hasn't,' spluttered Jamie. She doesn't exist!'

'But Jamie, in a funny sort of way she *does* exist,' said Mrs Nutbeam.

His father grinned. 'My sister is quite a girl! She's begun to live a life of her own!'

'That's the trouble,' said Jamie. 'She seems to be doing things we don't know about.'

While they were talking, the telephone rang. Dr Nutbeam was no longer grinning when he came back from answering it. 'That was Frank Figgis from the local paper.'

'Frank, the editor?' asked Mrs Nutbeam. 'What did he want?'

'He wants to do a full page feature on our Millicent,' groaned her husband. 'He's heard that she's about to set out on a climbing expedition in the Andes! Up some peak that has never yet been conquered!'

'What nonsense!' snapped Grandma. 'She's too old for that sort of thing.'

'It's just a rumour!' shouted Jamie. 'Who said she's going to the Andes? *I* didn't say she was going there. She's still in the Cameroons!'

'Calm down, dear,' said his mother, 'and let's hear what Dad said to Frank Figgis.'

Dr Nutbeam was rubbing his head. 'I stalled for time—I said we'd not heard she was in the Andes, but that we'd make enquiries and let him know. Whatever happens, Millicent mustn't get into print. We'll all be up on a charge of false pretences or something!'

Jamie snorted. 'Well, if she's climbing an Ande, it might be best if she fell off and was never seen again.'

Nerissa shrieked, '*No!* She mustn't—she's our only aunt and we've only just got her!'

Mrs Nutbeam sighed. 'Listen, Jamie, perhaps the time has come to own up that Aunt Millicent is not real.'

'We can't do that!' wailed Jamie. 'Everyone would think we're loony ... and that Grandma's absolutely bonkers, knitting socks for an aunt who isn't there. And what about the mongoose? Anyway, I *can't* let Honky Tonks find out now—she'd never stop crowing and she'd be more awful than ever.'

Jamie decided to lay the whole problem of Aunt Millicent Nutbeam before Mr Starling, right up to her unexpected expedition to the Andes and Mr Figgis's plan to write a full page feature about her for the local paper. He finished by saying, 'I think I might have to kill her off.'

'That'd be a shame,' sighed Mr Starling. 'She's quite a lady, your aunt!'

'It would be pretty easy to get rid of her,' Jamie went on. 'In her sort of job she could sink into a quicksand, or be trampled by a herd of elephants, or something.'

Mr Starling shook his head violently. 'No, no—it would only make things worse if she died a bloodcurdling death like that. No-one would be likely to forget her if she was squashed flat by a stampeding elephant. She'd become more interesting than ever!'

'Well, she could die of something boring, like pneumonia,' said Jamie. 'Or ... will I have to own up that she isn't real?'

'Do you want to own up?'

'Not really. I'd feel stupid, and I specially don't want Angelica Tonks to know I invented an aunt.'

Mr Starling quite understood. 'I see! Anyway, a lot of people would be sad to discover that Millicent Nutbeam was a hoax. The girls in your class, for example—she means a lot to them.'

'What'll I do then?'

'If you want people to lose interest in her, you'll just have to make her less interesting. I think she should retire from exploring, for a start.'

'Aw, gee!' Jamie felt very disappointed. 'I suppose so. I'll see what they think at home.'

'What he means,' said Dr Nutbeam, when Jamie had repeated Mr Starling's advice, 'is that it's time my dear sister Millicent settled down.'

'I quite agree with that,' remarked Grandma, who was up to the sixth sock foot. 'She's not as young as she was, and it's high time she had some normal home life. I think she should get married, even though she's getting on a bit. Perhaps to a widower.'

'That sounds terribly boring,' yawned Nerissa.

'Well, that's what we need,' said Jamie, 'something terribly boring to make people lose interest.'

Grandma sniffed. 'In my day it would have been called a happy ending.'

'Well, I suppose it's a happier ending than being squashed by an elephant,' conceded Jamie.

'How about marrying her to a retired accountant who used to work for a cardboard box company?' suggested his father. 'That sounds pretty dull.'

'Good heavens, it's all rather sudden!' said Mrs Nutbeam. 'Last time we heard of her she was climbing the Andes!'

'No, she *wasn't*.' At last Jamie felt he had hold of Aunt Millicent again. 'That South American stuff was just a rumour. The postman started it because of the letter from Peru, and then the story just grew!'

Dr Nutbeam nodded. 'Stories seem to have a habit of doing that, and so do rumours! But we can easily squash this one about the Andes. I'll just explain about the World Dental Conference on plaque. I even have the letter to prove it.'

Dr Nutbeam called Frank Figgis on the phone. He explained about the letter from Peru and about the ridiculous rumour which the postman had started. 'In your profession, Frank,' he added sternly, 'you should be much more careful than to listen to baseless rumour. It could get you into all sorts of trouble! In any case, Millicent is giving up exploring to marry a retired accountant. She's had enough.'

Frank Figgis was fast losing interest. 'I see—well, sometime when she's in Australia, we could do an interview about her former life ... maybe.'

'Maybe, although she has no immediate plans to return here. I believe she and her husband are going to settle down in England—somewhere on the seafront, like Bognor.'

Jamie passed on the same information to his class-mates. The girls were shocked.

'She's what?'

'Getting married to an *accountant*?'

'She can't be!'

'How boring for her!'

'Where in the world is Bognor? Is there really such a place?'

Angelica Tonks smiled like a smug pussycat. 'See! Your Aunt Millicent is just like any other old aunt, after all!'

Jamie caught Mr Starling's eye. It winked.

Aunt Millicent Nutbeam retired, not to Bognor but to live quietly with her family. Nerissa still had wonderful dreams. Dr Nutbeam still brought home books about far-off places. The bloodstained spears remained on the wall and the mongoose on the shelf. Jamie and Nerissa still played the tom-tom and the bamboo flute.

Grandma Nutbeam's holiday came to an end and she packed up to return home. She left a parcel for Jamie. When he opened it, he found three pairs of khaki socks with dark blue stripes, and a card which said:

Dear Jamie,
Aunt Millicent won't have any use for these now that she has settled down, so you might as well have them for school camps. Isn't it lucky that they are just your size!
With love from Grandma.

My Bonnie Lies Over the Ocean

David was asleep, at last. Goliath was dozing, but on guard with both lanky ears and every bulging muscle. Although the television was rubbishing on, Josie had her eyes shut, contemplating the boredom of Saturday nights.

For Josie Saturday nights were almost always the same—being left at home with Goliath to look after David, while her parents sped off to the nearby pub bistro for their weekly outing. Even that was boring to Josie—why didn't they try somewhere different?

David was Josie's small brother. Goliath was the Basset Hound and not as big as he sounded, but he sounded enormous through the front door, so Josie wasn't nervous—just peevish.

At three minutes past nine the telephone rang. Josie

heaved herself up and zapped the television before answering. It wouldn't be for her—all her friends would be out celebrating Saturday night.

'Hello?' she sighed.

'Halloo! An' whu is it I'm speakin' tu?'

Josie didn't recognise the voice. 'Who's that?' There were strange pauses on the line.

'Ma neem's Fairrgus.'

'Pardon—who?'

'F-E-R-G-U-S,' he spelled out. 'Fairrgus McPhee, that's ma neem.'

Josie had never heard of him. 'You must have the wrong number. Who d'you want to speak to?' she asked, rather impatiently.

'Och, just anyone. Ye'll du fine! What's *your* neem?'

'Well ... it's Josephine. I'm called Josie.' Goliath began growling, very low, as if warning Josie never to reveal her name to strangers like that.

'Halloo Juicy, it's grrand to talk wi' ye,' enthused Fergus McPhee.

'But why are you ringing?'

'Och, I jist felt like havin' a wee wurrd wi' someone. I'm lyin' here in ma bed with a leg in plaster an' ev'ryone else has gone oot, but they left the phuin by the bed in case I felt luinely!'

'But why did you phone us ... *me*?'

'Ah weel, I jist closed m' eyes and kept on pressin' dial numbers until something clicked and someone answered, and it was you! Ma fingerrs were guided that way, d'ye ken! And wheer d'ye live, Juicy?'

'In Sandringham.' She wished he wouldn't call her Juicy.

Goliath's growl was moving up the scale. Josie clamped her hand over the mouthpiece and hissed, 'Shut up dog. He doesn't know my surname or the street, does he!'

'Sandringham!' marvelled Fergus McPhee. 'So it's a Norfolk number I've dialled, is it. I suppoose the Queen is y'rr neighbour then, from time to time, when she has a holiday break. And is it chill and wintry doon theer?'

'No, it's boiling hot and I'm not in Norfolk.' This Fergus person must be a lunatic. Josie tried to think where Norfolk was. Somewhere in England, most likely, if the Queen had a holiday place there.

Fergus persisted. 'No' in Norfolk? Wheer then?'

'In Melbourne.'

'But ye said Sandringham. That's in Norfolk. Melbourne's in Derrbyshire.'

'This one's not, it's in Australia.'

'*Austreeliya*! Ye mean *that* Melbourne! Eeeh! This call will be costing poonds and poonds!'

'Well, you should have thought of that before you started fiddling around with the phone. Anyway, where are you ringing *from*?'

'Scotland!' came the wail. 'We live in Montrose!'

'Unreal! *Scotland*! That explains why you're called Fairrgus and why you say "poonds and poonds"!' Josie felt peevish no longer—this was really cool! 'Are you wearing tartan pyjamas?' she asked.

'I most sairrt'nly am not. They are blue with white stripes. Och, but will ye tell me how oold ye are?'

'I might if you'll tell me how you broke your leg ... and how old *you* are.'

'Weel, I'm fufteen ... an' ... I tripped over ma father's bagpipes.' There was a faint snort from Scotland.

'I bet you didn't—I don't *believe* you! Anyway, I'm fourteen.'

'That's just fine then! And actually I fell off ma bike. It skidded on the icy road last week and I near-ly cam to ma end under a bus.'

87

'Wow! I'm glad you didn't.'

'Are ye? Ye dinna even know me.'

'Yes I do, Fergus McPhee, I know quite a lot about you now, and later I'll look up Montrose on the map and see where you live.'

'The wind comes shriekin' across the North Sea at us, and sometimes th' old toon reeks o' fish a bit!'

'Are you by the sea too, then? So are we! Sandringham is on the edge of the Bay, Port Phillip. It's just a suburb really, but there are red cliffs, and *our* cold wind comes whooshing up from the Southern Ocean in winter.' Josie rarely thought about the red cliffs or the stiff winds, but suddenly she realised they were part of her life and she wanted to tell Fergus about them.

'There—we have a lot in common, see? Quick, let's write doon each other's phuin numbers—otherwise, all those poonds and poonds will have been wasted!'

They swapped the numbers and area codes.

'We'll need to find th' International codes too, in the d'rairct'ry,' Fergus told her.

Goliath was staring at Josie with deeply sorrowful eyes. 'Goliath is very suspicious of you,' giggled Josie.

'And whu on airrth's Goliath?'

'Our ace guard dog. He's a Basset and he and I mind David on Saturday nights when the parents go out on their weekly rage. David's my kid brother. He's four and he's mostly a pain.'

'David and Goliath, that's a hoot!' crowed Fergus. 'Hang on a wee minute ...'

There was a scuffling sound and then a strangled bark came down the line. Goliath rose up, growling terribly, and tried to eat the phone.

'Get *down*, Goliath, you idiot!' Josie shot to her feet holding the phone out of his reach. 'Who was that?' she asked.

'Hee! Tha' was ma friend Macduff. He's on the bed wi' me, nurrsin' me better. He's a Cairn terrier, ye ken.'

'Goliath would swallow him up.'

'I doot tha'—Macduff is a fearless wee creature, aren't ye, laddie?'

There were sounds of yapping and slapping and slurping from Scotland. In Sandringham, Goliath lay down with a deep sigh of despair.

'Will we talk again?' asked Josie, shyly.

'I tell ye what,' said Fergus, 'I'll be restin' ma leg by the phuin this time next week, and if ye want to ring me ... weel, I'd like it fine!'

Mum and Dad were bright and talkative when they came in, but yawny.

'Hello, Josie,' they called as they climbed over Goliath, who was at the front door making sure they weren't disguised housebreakers. 'Everything okay?'

'Aye ... I mean yup.'

'Thanks for sitting, love—it was great to get out. Any calls?'

'Just a wrong number—well, a sort of wrong number. It was a boy from Montrose. He's in bed with a broken leg, and we had this crazy talk.'

'Poor fellow,' yawned her dad. 'What did you talk about?'

'Oh, I dunno—about his leg, and where we live and things.'

'It's pretty up at Montrose ...' Her mum was yawning too. 'Mind you, I wouldn't want to live there in the bushfire season, all hemmed in by gum trees, with the mountain at the back—still, it's beautiful at other times of year.'

'Sure, once you're past the quarry and the factory belt,' said Mr Middleton.

Josie opened her mouth and shut it again, but *she* wasn't yawning—just stunned. They had homed in on Montrose in the Melbourne hills, the Dandenongs! Cool it, she told herself. No need to mention Scotland and send them into shock just yet. She used her off-hand voice. 'The boy gave me his number—I might ring him back sometime to see if his leg's better.'

'Hmm,' said her mother. 'What's this boy's name?'

'Fergus McPhee.'

'Whew! I bet he has porridge for breakfast!' grinned Mr Middleton. 'Would his people be from Scotland by any chance?'

'Could be, I s'pose,' mumbled Josie vaguely, scooping up her things and heading for her room. 'G'night.'

Josie lay smiling in the dark, mouthing 'Fairrgus McPhee' and 'poonds and poonds' to herself and hugging the spare pillow. Of all the billions of telephone numbers in the world, his fingers had picked out hers! Just one or two different digits could have connected him with an insurance company in Japan, or a fish-market in Argentina, or woken up some furious grand-mother in Mexico City—but no, his call came to *her*, Josie Middleton in Australia, who was about the same age and spoke the same language (almost) and was just as bored as he was until the phone rang.

It had to be a miracle.

Next morning she informed the family that she was seriously behind with her homework. This was nearly always true. She shut her bedroom door against raids by David and Goliath and set about some extensive research.

Her first resource was the telephone directory. At the front was an index which led her to a page headed International Direct Dial. First, it told her, she would have to dial 0011, the International Access Code, and then the Country Code. Her heart dropped to the pit of her stomach when she couldn't find Scotland on the alphabetical list of countries. Nor England, nor Wales, nor Great Britain ... what had happened to them all? Had they changed their names like African countries were always doing? Anxiously she ran her finger down the list, starting with A. She had nearly reached the end when, phew! relief! there it was—United Kingdom, code 44.

So, she'd have to dial 0011 plus 44 plus the area code and the local number Fergus had given her. It was a huge string of figures, about sixteen—she'd never keep them in her brain. Carefully Josie copied all the figures down on a small piece of paper and hid it in an old shoe at the back of her cupboard. Then she whisked the phone book back to the living room before it was missed, and pulled the big atlas off the shelf.

'How's it going?' asked Mum, who was passing through with a pot-plant. 'Maps today, is it?'

'Yup. Geog. homework.'

But this was a different, dreamy sort of geography.

Scotland. There it was, teetering on top of England like an oversized head on a squat body. Fergus would probably say that was because all the brains were in Scotland. She peered at England until she found Norfolk—it was the fat rumpy bit on the right, just asking for a slap on the bottom! No sign of the Norfolk Sandringham—the map was too small.

She found a larger map of Scotland by itself. To the west was the Atlantic Ocean and on that side the coast seemed to be all broken up and floating away, like icebergs, except the pieces were islands with weird names like Mull and Skye and Eigg and Rum. On the east side the coast had kept its hard edge and the sea was clear and empty, not littered with islands. The North Sea—that was the one Fergus had mentioned, the one the wind shrieked across. She ran her finger up the long meandering coast and there it was— Montrose, clinging to the edge! There was nothing between it and the bottom of Norway to screen it from the wind.

Later in the day she walked down to the cliff top to look at the Bay through her new eyes. The traffic roared along Beach Road behind her. To the left was the Red Bluff with the old ship's hulk half submerged just beyond. As she walked in the other direction, the city skyscrapers came into view above the shore like giant, uneven fangs glinting in the sun. Container ships and tankers lay hazily at anchor off the port, while closer to Sandringham little clusters of racing yachts breezed around their courses through the crinkled blue water. A few people were swimming and sailboarding at the beach below and a black dog bounded down a cliff path. The warm sea air washed softly over Josie's skin—there were no cold southerlies now, in late summer.

She gazed out at the enormous stretch of Port Phillip Bay. Would Fergus gaze across the grey blustery North Sea sometime today? Could he see it from his window? She had read about people putting messages in bottles and flinging them into the ocean. Supposing she sent Fergus a bottled message, would it ever float as far as the North Sea? No, that would be a hundred times more miraculous than Fergus choosing her phone number out of the whole world. If she threw a bottle into the sea off Sandy, it would probably wash up on the next beach down the Bay and some dork in Beaumaris or Mordialloc would find it and read her private message to

Fergus, or else the bottle would smash on the rocks and cut some innocent beachcomber's foot to ribbons. She shook herself free of that silly romantic daydream and thanked her lucky stars for telecommunications.

Suddenly, Saturday nights were no longer the dismal low point of the week—next Saturday had become the target of her whole existence! Nothing must stop her parents from going to the bistro. What if David caught chickenpox or Dad collapsed with gastric flu? She refused to think about it. Nothing must go wrong. Her parents *had* to be out on Saturday at 9 p.m.

What would she talk to Fergus about? Should she make a list of topics so as not to waste a micro-second of those hideously expensive minutes? Well—she knew nothing about his family. She could ask about them and how his leg was, and by then the time would be up. She'd already decided that two minutes would be the limit—that would add only about three or four dollars on to the phone bill, which wouldn't really be noticeable she supposed.

Nothing went wrong on Saturday night until six minutes to nine. Then David, who had been heavily asleep since 8.25, woke up with a wail and was spectacularly sick all over the doona.

Josie tried not to scream. 'Why did you have to pig out on ice-cream and caramel sauce, kid, tonight of all nights! Yuk!'

David just blubbered. It took ages to clean him up and change the doona cover and stop him crying, and she kept tripping over Goliath, who had stationed himself right in the way beside David's bed just to make sure that she did the job properly. Goliath was in charge.

Fortunately David fell heavily asleep again as soon as the clean-up was completed and Josie had put all the dirty things to soak in the laundry. '*Please* don't do it again,' she groaned to the sleeping body, 'not while I'm ringing Scotland!' She hoped it was just the ice-cream and not a gastric bug planning to launch a sneak attack every ten minutes.

By now she was badly flustered and not feeling nearly steady enough to make her first international phone call. She looked at the clock—it was already 9.22! Fergus would have given up waiting by now—he'd have decided she didn't want to talk to him after all, ever again.

Quick! She grabbed the crumpled piece of paper from her pocket, lifted the receiver, took six deep breaths and then began dialling before she had time to think. She followed the string of numbers on the paper and tried to pretend that this was an ordinary local call. 0011 ... 44 ... but how could it be like a local call, when every number carried her closer to Montrose, on the opposite side of the planet?

With a gasp, she reached the last digit. There was silence, then a click, then a bright little tune of computerised beeps, then more silence. She knew it—her phone call had been sucked into outer space! She felt almost relieved, but then ... brrr-brrr, brrr-brrr ... it was ringing in Fergus's house! Josie's mouth was dry. She heard a clatter as the receiver was lifted.

'Halloo?' It was a *woman's* voice!

Josie panicked and nearly dropped the phone, but she found herself saying, automatically, 'Hallo ... could I speak to Fergus please?'

'Just a mooment ... whu is tha' speaking?'

'Um ... my name is Josie.'

'Och, aye—ye'll be the wee lassie from Sandringham?

94

Fairrgus told us abuit his wrong number! D'ye ken, I've nivver set fuit in Norfolk!'

Josie was speechless, but the voice went on, 'Fairrgus is coming, but he'll be a wee moment managing his crutches.'

'I'm just ringing to see how his leg is,' faltered Josie.

'That's kind o' ye, Juicy. He's duin quite well, really.'

The precious seconds were flying past—it must be nearly a dollar's worth already. Then she heard his voice.

'Thanks Mither ... halloo? Is it you Juicy?'

'Yes, it's me. I'm sorry I'm late but beastly David was sick everywhere just when I was ready to ring!'

'Oh guid! I mean, it's guid that ye've called noo. I thought ye wer'na going to.'

'Did you want me to?'

'I sairrt'nly did—I've been awaitin' it all the week!'

'Me too! Was that your mum? It was a bit of a shock when she answered.'

'Aye—she beat me to the phuin while I was trippin' over ma crutches.'

'She thinks I live in Norfolk!'

'Aye, so she does. I jist told her Sandringham, and she jumped to the Norfolk conclusion, like I did.'

'Same here—I told my folks you live in Montrose, and they think you're only about thirty kilometres away, in the Dandies!'

'In the what?'

'The Dandenongs—some mountains just outside Melbourne. There's a Montrose there too, in the foothills!'

'That's amazin'. What's it like?'

'Not a bit like your Montrose. It doesn't smell of fish. It's got gum trees and winding roads I think, but

I've never been there.' Josie remembered her list of questions. 'But tell me about your family,' she said.

'Weel, ye've spoken to ma mither. Ma father's a teacher—kairmistry, w'd ye believe, and I'm the biggest duffer at it. An' I have two big sisters. One lives and wurrks in Dundee and the other one's married wi' two bairns.'

'Gee, you're an uncle already!'

'Aye, that I am, wi' two nephews! Is Goliath there noo?'

'He's sitting on my feet and disapproving of this phone call. How's Macduff?'

She heard Fergus whistle and then a huffing sound. Goliath was already standing up, rumbling in his throat.

'Stop it, Goliath—just say *Hi* to Macduff. It's not every dog gets a chance like this—*go on*!' Josie prodded her hound in the ribs. Goliath uttered one deep fruity bark, then lay down in embarrassment. There was a frantic yapping from Montrose.

'There—they've made contact. Dogs of the wurrld unite!' cried Fergus.

Josie told him she'd found Montrose on the map of Scotland. 'Can you see the North Sea from your place?' she asked.

'Noo, but we get a wee glimpse o' the Basin ... that's a sort o' lagoon wheer the river joins the sea. I found your Bay on the map, too. It's *huge*!'

'Yes, I s'pose it is. We can't always see the other side, only on clear days—or down to Arthur's Seat. That's a mountain right down near the other end of the Bay.'

'Y' dinna tell me ye have an Arthur's Seat—so have we! It's a big hill in Edinburgh, ye ken, wi' grrand views over the city and across the Firth o' Forth. I bet yours is named efter ours, by some puir homesick Scotsman ...'

'Probably—but quick, tell me about your leg.'

'Weel, I'll be limpin' back to schuil next week on ma crutches. Ma plaster cast is totally covered in graffiti already—there's not one white patch left anywheer. I think I might frame it when it comes off!'

Goliath was growling again and Josie remembered to look at the time. They'd been talking for five minutes already and they'd hardly said anything! The minutes would be adding up to seven or eight dollars!

'Help!' she croaked, 'I'll have to stop. We've been over five minutes—it'll be costing poonds and poonds!'

'Aye—maybe next time we'd better swap addresses,' said Fergus. 'My turn next week—have a wee pencil ready. Same time, eh Juicy?'

'Oh, aye—same time! G'bye!'

Josie hung up and sat there glowing. Goliath had closed his accusing eyes and David was still bombed out. She could sit there and relive her conversation with Fergus McPhee.

What did she know about him, after just two phone calls? He was fifteen and he lived in Montrose, a town with a shrieking wind and a fishy smell and a lagoon. His dad was a science teacher and his mum sounded okay, and he had two older sisters and two nephews. He also had a broken leg and graffiti on his cast, he wore striped pyjamas, used crutches, rode a bike, and had a wee dog called Macduff. Those were facts.

What else? Well, he had a great sense of humour and a *cute* voice. The boys she knew didn't talk like Fergus—they mostly grunted. Fergus was interesting and easy to talk to. She'd even found out things about her own part of the world, just chatting to him.

She suddenly realised this was the first time she'd made a friend without knowing what he looked like. What *did* he look like? No, she didn't want to know that just yet in case she was disappointed. He might be a weed, with thick glasses or buck teeth.

If they started writing letters, maybe they'd exchange photos. Which photo of herself would she send him? There weren't many. The one on the lawn with Goliath was quite good of her face, but she was wearing that prehistoric dress which Grandma had made. (The photo had been taken for Grandma, just to prove that Josie was wearing the thing.) The school photo made her eyes look black and it showed up every pimple, especially that giant one she'd had on her nose.

Josie sighed. What you *looked* like could so easily put people off. She could think of kids at school she didn't bother about because they didn't look right. What was 'right', anyway? Wearing bands on your teeth, or a daggy haircut, or the wrong brand of jeans was not 'right'. Being fat and shapeless or too short or being hopeless at hockey, wasn't 'right'. Things like that put you off people, so you never got to know them.

Making friends with Fergus was different—she was getting to know him without even thinking about what he was wearing or what he looked like. She didn't want a photo yet. She wanted to know him better first, the real Fergus underneath.

Josie went back to the cliff top after school one day, to sniff the sea air and to see if Arthur's Seat was visible. Yes, the mountain was floating there between sea and sky, in a watercolour of blues. They'd been down there last year and ridden up in the chairlift. The view from the top was better than being in a plane—you could see right down to the Heads and to the ocean out past the long jawline of the Peninsula. Container ships sat like matchboxes on the silvery Bay, and the boats from different yacht clubs could have been flights of wispy moths feeding on the surface. She'd had to remind herself that the tiny toy houses clustered along the shore and at the foot of the mountain had real people, families, in them. She'd felt no bigger than a speck of dust up there, with the huge world spread out below.

Casually, Josie began to drop the name of 'Fergus' into conversations at school, and she soon became a centre of curiosity among the girls. She thought it best to remain mysterious for the time being and not to mention Scotland. Having a boyfriend on the far side of the planet probably wouldn't count as the real thing. But she told them about the 'wrong number' and her chance meeting with Fergus on the phone. Everyone agreed it was a miracle and dreamily romantic. Josie played up the seriousness of Fergus's injured leg, too, adding a severed Achilles tendon and bunches of torn ligaments, so that he could be conveniently immobilised for ages and they wouldn't expect her to produce him at parties.

'Anyway, he lives a long way off,' she said, 'you know, right over the far side.'

They sympathised with her for having a boyfriend on the other side of vast, sprawling Melbourne—he was geographically very difficult. More like geographically hopeless, Josie thought to herself.

'Oh well,' she sighed stoically, 'we'll just have to be phone friends for a while.'

'Poor you,' said the envious girls.

There was that other worry—the cost of the international phone calls. Her parents were niggly enough when she made local calls to her friends, and they kept telling her not to hog the line and send the phone bill rocketing into the National Debt zone. If they knew she was ringing Scotland once a fortnight they'd probably lock her up. They'd certainly forbid her from ringing Fergus, or else they'd stand over her while she talked to make sure she stopped after one minute flat. Either way would be a disaster. She just loved talking privately to Fergus and hearing his cute voice and hearing Macduff yapping to Goliath and all those things. Writing letters would be so dreary and slow. A FAX would be better, but they didn't have one.

When would the next telephone account arrive? She would have to research the household bills. There was time on Saturday night, after getting her parents off to the bistro and David into bed and before Fergus rang at nine.

The household accounts, after they'd been paid, were stuffed into a folder in one of the cupboards near the phone. Josie pulled them out and spread them all over the carpet. Goliath lay down next to her looking more sorrowful than ever at her deceitful ways. The accounts were all higgledy, but after sorting through several dozen she found a telephone bill, dated January. She delved further and further back until two more came to light—October and July.

'Okay dog,' she said to Goliath, 'this could be where Applied Maths has its uses,' and counting on her fingers she worked out that the next quarterly account should land in the letterbox in early April. Just over a month away—and including two more phone calls to Montrose from her end.

She tried to decipher the accounts. Would there be any evidence to give her away? Like, *Calls to Montrose, Scotland* listed on certain dates? Her parents never made overseas calls, so it was a bit hard to tell from these accounts—but, wait a minute, last Christmas they *had* rung the grandparents who were holidaying in California. Yes, Josie remembered her mum going into a panic about the cost and her dad saying, 'Rubbish—it won't hurt this once. The phone's there to be used, so let's use it!' Ha! He'd actually said that!

She checked the January account and found a list of Call Charges. At the bottom of the list it said

```
0011 IDD International—see over for details.
```

Josie flipped the page and felt herself flushing hot. Every detail of the Christmas call to California was recorded there—the date, the time, the place and the number, the length of the call in minutes and seconds, and the cost—$6.40! She was trapped!

She grabbed on to her father's remark—'The phone's there to be used, so let's use it!' Right, Dad! Except, of course, kids don't count. In the end, as usual, it was just a matter of money. Dad wouldn't mind her using the phone if it was free. She could ring the North Pole three times a day, if it was free. Maybe if she could find the money to pay for her calls, she wouldn't be locked up or forbidden to ring Fergus.

She'd forgotten the time as she brooded, so she jumped clean out of the chair when the phone rang. She lunged at it. Four minutes to nine—Fergus was early!

'Halloo!' she cried, mimicking his voice.

'Is that you Josie? It's Auntie Edie here, dear.'

Josie sank despairingly into the chair. Great-aunt Edie, the world's champion gasbag, who rang once a month with the latest instalment of her life story, minute by minute, interspersed with moans about the trials of old age.

'Hi, Auntie Edie,' she answered, bleakly. 'Mum and Dad are out to dinner—can they ring you back?'

'Oh, never mind dear, just give them a few messages from me will you? Now, first of all, I'm having trouble with the drain under the kitchen sink, and I don't have the right tools to undo the U-trap, and even if I did I couldn't use them with my arthritis. Old age is very cruel, you know dear ...'

Josie's hair was on end. What could she do to throttle Aunt Edie before she really got launched? If only David had chosen *this* week to throw up at three minutes to nine, it would have been the perfect let-out— but David's gastric system was quite normal again and he was deeply asleep. So was Goliath. Phone calls from Aunt Edie didn't excite Goliath in the slightest. Josie tried rib-tickling him with her foot to make him bark, so that she could tell Aunt Edie there was someone at the door, but the rotten dog just rolled out of reach—and Auntie surged on.

'... and another thing, tell your mother that my nice girl at the hair salon has left to have a baby, which is very thoughtless of her, because there's just no-one else at that place who understands my hair ...'

Josie wasn't surprised that no-one understood it, and she was so busy picturing Aunt Edie's pink-tinted frizz that she completely missed the message for her mother, and by the time she'd tuned in again, Auntie was on to the scandalous price of mid loin chops.

Josie's panic was rising. It was nearly 9.15 and Fergus would be losing patience—he'd probably think she was on the line chattering to some local hero, having quite forgotten that he, Fergus McPhee, would be ringing. And the living room floor looked like a tip, littered with all the household bills. Would she have time to tidy them away into the cupboard before her parents arrived home? However could she explain the mess to them?

At 9.20 she detected a slight pause in Aunt Edie's monologue, and she managed to slide herself into the gap.

'Okay, Auntie Edie—I'll tell them you rang and they'll probably ring you back tomorrow to arrange about fixing the drain. G'night!'

Josie jammed down the receiver before the old lady had a chance to rewind. She fell on her knees and began to scoop up the scattered accounts, but almost immediately the phone rang once more. Ow! Please not Auntie Edie again to say she'd forgotten something! But no, it was Fergus.

'Halloo, Juicy?—I couldna get through!'

'Sorry—my great-aunt beat you to it and she always puts on this great steamroller performance. I didn't know how to terminate her!'

'Whew! Weel, even steamrollers run out o' steam in th' end. Hoo are things duin under?'

'Fine, okay—well, just about. The floor's covered with bills—I've been trying to work out when the next phone account is due, and it's in April. And every detail of calls to Montrose will be on it!'

'So ...?'

'I'm a bit worried about the poonds and poonds—you know, if the phone bill blows out because of calls to Scotland, Dad might stop me ringing.'

'I've told ma pairents about you being in Austreeliya,' said Fergus.

'What did they *say*?' gasped Josie.

'No' a wurrd at furrst—they were too flabbergasted!

And then ma father began splutterin' aboot the poonds, but I told him I'd pay for the international calls m'sel! Then Mither went all soft and said it was a marvel I'd dialled someone like you, when it could ha' been the local gasworks! She's a wee bit romantic.'

'I know!' cried Josie. She knew Mrs McPhee was okay—she would understand about miracles. 'How are you going to earn the money?' she asked.

'I've offered m'sel as a reliable baby-sitter for those wee nephews, now and again, at moderate rates—just as soon as ma plaster's off. Ye gave me th' idea, looking efter wee David every Saturday. And Mither says she'll subsidize the phuin calls until I'm fit again— she's still grateful I didna end up under the bus, ye ken. But listen, have ye a pencil ready—to swap addresses, remember?'

Josie had forgotten in her confusion, so she had to hunt for writing gear, and by the time they'd sorted out their postal addresses and written them down and checked them back the time was marching on to 9.30.

'Hoots, I mun go—the poonds are pilin' up!' said Fergus. 'Mither says will ye send a photo?'

'I s'pose so—will you?'

'If ye want it.'

Josie wasn't sure that she did want it yet, but it would have been difficult to explain why, so she said yes.

She left the accounts on the floor, stacked into rough piles. Mr and Mrs Middleton were usually mellow after the bistro, so this was as good a time as any to confess.

After the opening parental outburst about the mess, Josie said, 'I needed to find out how the phone accounts work.'

Goliath had almost tripped Mr Middleton up at the

door, so her father's adrenalin was pumping.

'What on earth for?' he snapped. 'Are you doing a Telecom project?'

'Not really ... I just thought it would be best if I paid for my calls to Fergus McPhee.'

'For goodness sake ... how often do you ring him?'

'Every second Saturday, just for a few minutes.'

Mrs Middleton melted. 'Isn't that sweet—that's very thoughtful, Josie, but really, one call a fortnight to Montrose will hardly be noticed on the phone bill. It's just a local call, you know.'

'Well, *your* Montrose is, but actually Fergus lives in another Montrose. The one in Scotland.'

'In Scot ... *SCOTLAND*!!' bellowed her father.

Goliath rolled his eyes and slunk into the passage. Mrs Middleton fell into the couch. The room was silent while everyone adjusted to this new world picture.

Mr Middleton's adrenalin was now foaming, but Mrs Middleton started to laugh. She flopped back against the cushions and indulged in a mild attack of hysterics. Goliath waddled back and sat beside her anxiously.

'That's why I'm offering to pay for the phone calls,' explained Josie when her mother had quietened down a bit. 'Fergus is paying for his—he's earning the money by baby-sitting, so I thought ... maybe ...'

There was a further silence as more mental adjustments took place. Mr Middleton was frowning heavily over closed eyes, but it was mostly a sign of concentration after a good dinner. Eventually he spoke.

'Right. Two hours baby-sitting every week—ten dollars. One measured call to Scotland every second week, say ten dollars. That leaves about ten dollars over each fortnight—might I suggest that you invest them in some airmail stamps and writing gear? How's that seem?'

Josie rushed at her father and bear-hugged him, then collapsed on the couch beside her mother for a smoodge. Goliath was panting with relief.

'Seems like a fair bargain,' yawned Mrs Middleton, 'and you yourself said the phone was there to be used, dear,' she reminded her husband. Secretly, to herself, she was thinking, *Josie is much safer here talking to that boy in Scotland than she would be out on the town in some unroadworthy car. Long may it last!*

Mr Middleton was smiling, now that the financial problem had been solved, and he began to sing an old song, very softly ... *My Bonnie lies over the ocean, My Bonnie lies over the sea ...*

Flushing hot, Josie climbed out of the couch and went to bed.

Josie chose to send Fergus the photo of herself on the lawn with Goliath, in spite of the prehistoric dress. She thought he'd be more interested in Goliath than the dress, and her own face looked almost passable in this picture.

It was nearly two weeks before Fergus's first letter arrived. It was all decorated with glowing stamps and airmail stripes, like a jewel shining among the drab local envelopes and junk mail in the letterbox.

There was a photograph enclosed, but she kept it face down until she'd read Fergus's letter and the tourist brochure about Montrose which he'd sent to show pictures of the Basin thronged with wild birds wading on the tidal flats, and a sandy beach stretching along the edge of the North Sea (which looked blue in the photograph). There were people playing golf and others outside an antique shop in a street lined with handsome stone buildings, and there were pictures of boats in a harbour. The sun shone cheerfully in every

106

picture and the brochure didn't mention the cold winds or the icy roads which had catapulted Fergus off his bike.

Then, forgetting to breathe, Josie turned the snapshot over. On the back was scrawled 'Taken last summer'. Fergus stood there against a grey stone wall, grinning at her. He was in shorts and open shirt, and he was tall and his eyes twinkled, but, whichever way Josie looked at him—and she tried all ways, even upside down—he was *ugly*! He seemed to be all bone and joints and ears, with a long scrawny neck poking from his shirt collar, and reddish hair standing on his head in a thick crop, and his grinning mouth was wide and toothy. She wouldn't be taking this photograph to school, no way. But somehow he was still gorgeous, because she knew more about him than any photo could tell.

Rather reluctantly Josie showed the photo to her mother. Mrs Middleton broke into a smile.

'What a character!' she exclaimed. 'Oh, he'll turn into a bonny Scotsman when he all grows together. Give him three years to fill out and he'll be like a grand Highland crag!'

Josie wasn't sure that a grand Highland crag was what she wanted, but she did know that Saturday night couldn't come soon enough, when she would hear him lift the receiver and say, 'Halloo ... and is it you, Juicy?'

Bate

Mrs Beamish drives our school bus. She teaches craft at school, and she plays the piano and helps with the class singing, too. When she heard that the school needed a bus driver for our route, she offered to do it. She's that sort of person. It meant having special training and going for a driving test, and when she came back to school after the test she was all whoopee and stood in the middle of the yard saying, 'Heaven help me! I'm a *bus* driver, would you believe!'

Mr Beamish is the shire engineer and they bought this place about three kilometres past our farm when they first came here, because they wanted to live out of town on a few hectares of their own.

The Beamishes live at the end of the route and our

farm is next along, so I'm always first on to the bus in the mornings and last off in the afternoons and Mrs Beamish and I have a bit of time to talk. It's five kilometres before we pick up the next bunch of kids and you can talk quite a lot in five Ks. Mrs Beamish is interested in everything and she's always asking questions about the farms and who lives in them, and about crops and animals, because she grew up in the city and she still has a lot to learn about the country. Sometimes I have to remind myself that *she* is meant to be the teacher!

Still, she often says something I'd never thought of before about things I've known all my life. Once she looked at some cockatoos perched all over a dead gum tree in a paddock, and she said the tree looked like a huge branched candlestick filled with white candles. And she thought the parrots zipping past the bus were like streaks of paint. She asked me why many Australian birds were coloured like stained glass while our animals are all brown and earthy. I didn't really know—I'd never thought about it.

One day when I climbed into the bus I was whistling a tune. It was one of those tunes you get on the brain and it takes about two days to clear it out. I'd heard this one on a television commercial which they'd played about twenty times during a programme the night before, driving us all crazy.

'Hi, Mrs Beamish,' I said, shooting my bag under the front seat, and I went on whistling while she got the bus rolling again.

After a bit she said, 'That's Beethoven.'

I stopped whistling. 'Pardon?'

'That tune you're whistling—it's Beethoven.'

'Bate who?'

'Hoven. He wrote the tune, composed it.'

109

Gee. Mrs Beamish didn't know much about farming, but she knew a lot of other things. How on earth
did she know who wrote this tune?

'Does he belong to some group?' I asked.

'Beethoven!' she exploded. 'He's only been dead
about 170 years!'

'Well, how could he have written this tune then? It
was on the WOOF-O dog food commercial last night,
you know, on telly.'

'Easy—they've pinched it. I can promise you that
Beethoven wrote that tune. It's part of one of his sym-
phonies.'

'What's a symph— ... what's that?'

'It's a long piece of music for orchestra.'

'Well, what I heard was a very short piece and it was
played on a synthesiser with some vocalists. It can't be
the same. Anyway, how do you know?'

'It's very famous. Millions of people all over the
world know that tune—even you know it now, or a bit
of it. The real tune is longer and a big choir sings it
with the orchestra.'

'As big as our school choir?'

'Heavens, about ten times bigger. They sing the
words of a poem called "Ode to Joy."'

'What did he owe to Joy, this Bate chap?'

Mrs Beamish shrieked again. 'No, not O-W-E-D,
silly, but O-D-E. An ode is a song or poem.'

'Okay, then who was Joy? Was she his girlfriend, or
his missus?' Bate and Joy Hoven, I was figuring they
would be, and he was writing her a poem. People did
things like that 170 years ago.

The bus lurched as Mrs Beamish let out another
squawk. She heaved on the wheel to get us back on a
steady track, and then she said, 'No, you've got it
wrong. It means Joy like happiness, being joyful, you

110

know—rapt. This Joy is a sort of goddess and the song is to her. She wasn't a human person—and anyway poor old Beethoven never had a missus.'

We slowed down to collect the next lot of kids. By then I realised that I'd forgotten the tune, anyway.

That afternoon when I was the last person left on the bus going home, Mrs Beamish handed me a card with a man's picture on it.

'That's him,' she explained. 'You know, Beethoven. I found it at school. There was a pile of old stuff in the music room.'

Fancy her still being on about Bate. I'd almost forgotten him. 'I can't even remember the tune any more,' I told her.

Straight off she sang it, but what she sang was about twice as long as the WOOF-O tune. Mrs Beamish had a loud, rich voice, and she waved one arm about and pounded the other hand on the steering wheel in time to the music. Luckily it was a straight piece of road.

'You're clever to remember it like that,' I said.

'Not really. It's so well-known I could never forget it.'

I looked at Bate's picture. He had a frowning, rather fierce face which reminded me of an angry bullock. You wouldn't want to get on the wrong side of him. His eyes were looking somewhere else, sort of into space. He would have been told to have his hair cut at *our* school, but he wasn't a weed—he looked strong and nuggety, as if he played footie.

Under the picture it said *Ludwig van Beethoven*. What a mouthful! If it was written *Beet* why was it pronounced *Bate*? I decided to stick with *Bate* anyway. Then it said *Born 1770 Bonn, died 1827 Vienna*. Almost back to the dinosaurs.

111

1770 rang a bell though. 'What happened in 1770, apart from Bate's birthday?' I asked Mrs Beamish.

'Don't tell me you've forgotten that!' she snorted. 'Remember Captain Cook?'

'*That's* right, Captain Cook arrived—I hadn't really forgotten,' I muttered. 'So ... um ... Bate was born over in Europe before there were any white people living in Australia, and now I bet the place is full of people with Bate's tune on the brain because they heard it on telly. That's pretty queer, isn't it.'

'I suppose *he'd* think it was queer,' agreed Mrs Beamish, 'but I'm sure he'd be pleased. He had all these ideas about everyone in the world getting on happily together. That's what the Ode to Joy is all about, really.'

'Gee,' I thought. 'The things you find out on the bus!'

The WOOF-O commercial was on television again that night and I listened to it more carefully so that I'd remember the words.

> *Our dogs love the taste of WOOF-O,*
> *Our dogs munch it every day,*
> *Our dogs won't eat any other—*
> *Why not buy some right away!*

Later I propped Bate's picture up beside my bed and looked at his frowning face. I wondered if he was a dog lover. He looked a bit like a bulldog himself.

Next morning I sang the words of the WOOF-O song to Mrs Beamish on the first leg of our journey.

'Ye gods!' she exploded, while the bus wobbled. 'That is *appalling*! Beethoven would turn in his grave!'

'What would he really think if he came back to life and saw the WOOF-O ad?' I wondered.

She thought for a moment. 'Well ... I suppose he'd be totally bewildered. He wouldn't know what canned pet food was, for one thing, let alone television or sound recording or synthesisers. All he'd recognise would be the dog!'

'And his own tune,' I added.

'Yes ... *NO*! I've just remembered that he was stone deaf! If he came back now he wouldn't even *hear* the WOOF-O song, thank goodness. I'd feel ashamed of modern civilisation if he heard *that* rubbish!'

It took me a second to take in what she'd said. 'Did you say deaf?' I gaped. 'Bate was deaf?'

'He was indeed, for about half his life, poor fellow.'

'Well, how did he make up tunes?'

'I suppose he could hear music inside his head, if you know what I mean. It must be the same if you go blind—I suppose you could still imagine the things you used to be able to see.'

I told Mrs Beamish about the time last year when I broke my leg and couldn't play football for ages. I could imagine what it *felt* like to play, even though I wasn't able to. It was awful having to sit there and watch the others tearing up and down the field on two good legs.

'At least your leg got better,' sighed Mrs Beamish. 'Beethoven just grew deafer and deafer. D'you know, after the first performance of this symphony he didn't even realise that the audience were clapping and cheering. Someone had to turn him round and show him.'

We stopped then for the next kids and I spent the rest of the trip trying to feel deaf. I blocked my ears with my fingers as hard as I could, but even so I could still hear the rumble of the bus very faintly. But I couldn't hear the other kids shouting and talking. I watched two of them across the aisle and tried to read their lips, but I was hopeless at it. There was a dull sort of hum in my head. I remembered Bate's face in the picture—his frown, his eyes looking lost. Lonely, that's how deaf people look, and that's how it felt, like being locked away from everything.

I visited the school library at lunchtime to see if there were any books about Bate. I don't know why, but I wanted to find out a bit more about him—not his music, but him. Bate was in a book called *Lives of Great Composers* so I borrowed it and read it in bed that night.

Gee—poor old Bate! His father was a drunk and his mum died when he was a teenager. After that Bate had to cope with his father and two young brothers and he hardly had any schooling after he was eleven. He was short and ugly and he never married anyone, like Mrs Beamish said, although it seems that he asked one or two. I suppose they thought he was too ugly. It sounds as if he needed someone to look after him, as he was scruffy and lived in a mess and never had enough money. On top of all that he went deaf. No wonder he had a frowning face—I think I would have given up, but Bate wrote all this music. Fancy him even thinking about Joy!

Mrs Beamish had a surprise for me next day. The bus had a cassette player in it and she slipped in a tape. Next minute the bus was full of music, very loud!

'Is this Bate's symphony?' I asked, after listening for a minute.

'Yes,' she shouted above the noise. 'I've wound the tape on to where the tune starts—it's in the last movement. Now listen, the choir will be coming in soon.'

Well, first there was a man singing the tune by himself and then the choir started. It sounded like a huge crowd at the Wembley Cup Final when they all start singing and shouting, but these were better than that because they were a proper choir. The bus was nearly bursting with noise and Mrs Beamish was waving a hand and bouncing around to the beat. It was pretty exciting—much better than the WOOF-O tune—but I hoped she would turn it off before the other kids got in. They'd think I was a weirdo listening to that sort of stuff.

She did switch it off as we rumbled up to the others waiting under their gum tree and everything was suddenly quiet and rather empty. I could still hear the tune in my head and then I knew what Mrs Beamish had meant about Bate being able to compose music even though he was deaf. I sang it to myself 'inside' and my foot beat time under the seat.

It was pretty amazing really—Bate had made up this tune in his head and 170 years later here I was singing it inside *my* head on a school bus in Australia, and nobody else on the bus even knew I was doing it—except maybe Mrs Beamish. I could see her hand beating time on the steering wheel and her head nodding about and I knew she was singing it too. I hoped we'd be able to listen to more of the tape on the way home when the others had all got out. Bate's tune sounded pretty good out there on the road with flocks of galahs bursting into the sky like pink star shells.

Staying with the Slingsbys

When the tractor rolled and crushed Dad's leg, I had to go and stay with the Slingsbys. Dad's leg was going to be all right, but he needed to be in hospital for a while and Mum wanted to be in town close to him. So I was packed off to the city. I offered to stay and look after the farm for them. I knew what to do, but they said heavens no, how could they leave a kid of twelve all alone like that? I suppose they were right—it would have been a bit lonely even with the dogs. Anyway, the neighbours on the next place promised to keep an eye on things and to feed the chooks and the dogs, and Mum would be able to drive out now and then to check. So off I went on the bus to the Slingsbys—Uncle Malcolm and Auntie Beryl and their kids. Mum and Auntie Beryl are sisters, but we didn't ever see the Slingsbys, or hardly at all, because they lived so far away and they never seemed to have time to come to the country. Perhaps they didn't want to.

I went to say goodbye to Dad in hospital when everything had been arranged. His leg was all plastered up and hurting, but even so he grinned as he said to me, 'I wonder how you'll get on with old Dizz!'

Dad always called Uncle Mal 'old Dizz' and I'd never thought about why, but now I wanted to know. 'Why do you call him that?' I asked.

'It was his nickname at school,' Dad explained. 'The other kids called him Dismal Slingsby because he was so gloomy. Dis Mal—get it? And then it was shortened to Dizz.'

Dis Mal. Pretty smart, I thought.

'Is he still gloomy?'

'I reckon,' sighed Dad. He looked at Mum. 'Do you remember when those youngsters of theirs were just babies, Dizz would say, "Poor little kids, I wonder what's to become of them?"'

Mum giggled. 'Yes, I remember, as if he expected them to be washed down the plughole after their next bath!'

Dad was chuckling, too, in spite of his leg. 'And you know, when those kids started crawling, old Dizz pulled most of the plants out of their garden in case they were poisonous!'

'And don't forget the two trees he chopped down in case the children fell out of them!' added Mum. 'He always fears the worst, does our Mal.'

Uncle Dizz sounded a bit mad to me. 'Is Auntie Beryl gloomy too?' I asked.

'Well, she was quite a cheerful person once, when we were girls,' Mum said, 'but I think living with a

117

gloomy person can be like living with someone who has influenza—it's catching, and I'm afraid Auntie Beryl might have caught it.'

'Oh heck!' I said, thinking of the weeks of gloom ahead of me. 'I wonder if I'll catch it too?'

'Not a chance,' said Dad. 'You're too bouncy, and anyway you won't be there very long. You'll be fine.'

'Gee, I hope so. Where do you think Uncle Mal caught it from?'

They both thought for a bit, and then Mum said, 'Probably from his mother, Granny Slingsby. Mal was only six when his dad died, you know, and after that his mother was a very nervous person, always worrying that everything would go wrong, and I don't blame her. So I expect Mal picked it up from her, poor thing.'

After that, I wasn't looking forward to the Slingsbys much and I wondered what the kids would be like and if they'd caught the glooms as well. There were two of them. Victor was older than me, about fourteen, and Rosie was just a bit younger.

The Slingsbys were very kind when I arrived—you know, filling me up with cake and things—but straightaway I saw what Mum and Dad meant.

Uncle Dizz looked at me sadly, like a spaniel, and sighed. 'Your poor father. I suppose this means he'll be crippled for life, does it?'

'Shush, dear,' said Auntie Beryl. 'Don't upset Sandy by talking about such things. We want this visit to be as happy as possible.'

Some chance, I thought to myself.

Uncle Dizz was in insurance. Each morning as he left for work, he would open the front door and then fire a parting gloom down the hall. 'Goodbye, I'm going early in case the train services are disrupted.' Or, 'I'm sure the forecast was wrong. I knew I should have worn a winter vest, but it's too late now.' Or, 'Do be careful of the car, dear. The traffic gets worse every day.'

So poor Auntie Beryl probably spent lots of time worrying in case Uncle Dizz was hours late for work, or catching a chill, or she was going to come home with a mangled mudguard or something. No wonder she'd forgotten how to be cheerful.

I couldn't understand it, really. Uncle Dizz didn't have much reason to be gloomy that I could see. I mean, at home there are always things to worry about, like droughts and fires and mouse plagues. Whenever there's a drought and the paddocks turn to grey dust, Dad just says, 'Things are pretty tough, but it'll have to rain again one day, nothing surer.' And Mum goes and plants extra vegetables and waters them with bath water and says, 'We won't starve, anyway, not if we can help it.' Uncle Dizz didn't have to cope with things like that, so he must have caught his glooms from Granny Slingsby, like Mum said.

I asked Auntie Beryl one day if he'd had any accidents in his life. We'd been talking about Dad and the tractor, so I just slipped the question in. I thought something might have happened to Uncle Dizz when he was younger which would explain why he was so jumpy now, something apart from his dad dying. You know, he could have been blown over a cliff or almost flattened by a diesel truck or electrocuted or something. But Auntie Beryl said no, he'd never broken any bone larger than his fourth finger and he'd never been seriously ill. She even said he'd had a very fortunate life! Well, Uncle Dizz seemed to be nervous that his luck wouldn't hold out much longer.

I slept in a small room next to Victor's. I don't think Victor noticed me much. His bedroom walls were covered with swanky pinboards and shelves full of folders and books, and there was a big desk all stacked with paper and neat plastic holders full of pencils, textas, rulers and things. On a smaller table there was a computer. I asked Victor what it was for, hoping he might let me play computer games.

'I do all my school assignments on it,' he said, 'and I'm doing an extra computer course after school, so I practise on this one.' He didn't mention games, not then or ever.

Victor wasn't gloomy really, but he didn't have much time to talk. He always seemed to be working. It was school holidays when I was there, but Victor was always flat out practising on his computer or doing school assignments or jogging round the park with a stopwatch to time his runs. He learnt the bassoon and honked away at that for hours, and he went to an Indonesian class on Thursday evenings and special golf lessons on Saturday mornings. That seemed a bit funny to me, because I'd always thought golf was for older people, but then Victor acted as if he wanted to be old. He must have been pretty clever, I suppose, but I didn't think I'd want to live my whole life boxed up like a school timetable.

Then I remembered that we had a sort of timetable on the farm, too, and that I was always pretty busy before and after school, helping with the jobs and feeding the animals. But there was still time to muck about and talk to people and play with the dogs. The Slingsbys didn't have a dog. No pets at all, not even a goldfish. 'Oh no,' said Uncle Dizz. 'You can pick up all sorts of things from pets. Not just fleas, but serious diseases, I mean.'

I felt like telling him what we had to do with some of the farm animals, like the time Dad showed me how to give the kiss of life to a newborn calf which seemed to be almost dead. I didn't like doing it much, blowing hard into one of its slimy nostrils, but it was terrific when the calf suddenly breathed, like a kick-start! I felt really good then and didn't mind the slime all over my face. I didn't catch anything, either. I decided to save that story up until I knew the Slingsbys a bit better. I didn't want anyone to faint.

But I did tell Rosie about hatching chickens under broody hens and what fun it was when the chickens started to chip their way out of the eggshells, and how when you lifted up the old hen one morning there would be this fluffy swarm of chicks with little bright eyes all looking at you.

Rosie liked that, but she said they weren't allowed to have any birds at their place. 'Dad says we might be allergic to feathers or get parrot's disease,' she explained. 'But I think that's *stupid*!'

I hadn't expected to find Rosie very interesting, but she was a real surprise, especially after Victor. Later I told Mum that I thought Rosie took after *our* side of the family and not the Slingsbys. She didn't seem to have caught the gloom germs. Maybe with a name like Rosie it was easier to stay cheerful.

Well, because Victor was always so busy improving himself, I spent most of my time with Rosie. Uncle Dizz wanted to enrol us both in a school holiday programme run by the local council. He said it would give me all sorts of 'opportunities' I didn't have at home, whatever that meant. The leaflet said we could choose what we'd like to do from a whole list of things. I couldn't believe some of them, like Low Fat Cooking for Kids, a Calligraphy Workshop and a Painting Clinic. I had to ask what Calligraphy was and the Painting Clinic sounded like a visit to the doctor. There were lots more too, and I wasn't sure what to think.

121

Maybe it would have been a good idea, because there wasn't much to do at the Slingsbys. You know, their garden and yard were all square and neat with lots of cement driveway and edges, and no decent trees because Uncle Dizz had chopped them down. And Auntie Beryl went out to work every afternoon, so I was wondering if we could fill in time by doing one of these programmes. Some of them weren't too way out, like Tennis Coaching and Karate, which I wouldn't have minded. Karate could probably be quite useful when you're dealing with bullocks.

But Rosie suddenly blew her top. She even stamped her foot. 'I don't *want* to do any programmes while Sandy's here!' she shouted. 'We're supposed to be on holiday, so why do we have to?'

The other three Slingsbys all looked sort of amazed. They were probably a bit embarrassed that Rosie was raving on like that in front of me.

Auntie Beryl said to her, 'We only want to do what's best for you, dear.'

'How do you *know* what's best for me?' roared Rosie.

'Now Rosie, don't shout at your mother like that and don't be silly,' said Uncle Dizz, who looked quite shaky. 'You children are so fortunate nowadays to have all these chances, to be able to do programmes like this.'

'*Why?*' yelled Rosie.

Wow! This was getting pretty interesting! I had a feeling that Rosie hoped I'd back her up, but I kept right out of the way and just listened. Victor was looking smug, thinking of his golf lessons, I bet.

Uncle Dizz had begun to turn red by now. '*Why?*' he repeated. 'Don't you *want* to get on?—to get an education? Courses like this are an investment in your future, you know!' That's what it had said on the leaflet, too.

'I'm *sick* of always thinking about my future,' said Rosie. 'What about *now*? What about my holidays?'

Well, Rosie was really stubborn and her mum and dad gave in. They said she needn't do a programme this time, because I was visiting, and we could do things together at home, as long as I didn't mind. I didn't mind really. I was a bit sorry about the Karate Course, but Uncle Dizz probably wouldn't have let me do it anyway, in case I broke my toe.

We took a little while to find things to do, things that we both liked. I said to her one day that I wished my dog Streak was with me, because I really missed him.

'I wish he was here too,' said Rosie. 'I wish I had a dog. Mr Mudge over the road has one. It's just a sleepy old labrador, but it's better than nothing if you want to see it. Mr Mudge is a bit sour, but I don't mind going over there if you'll come too.'

Rosie was right. Mr Mudge was a bit sour, what Dad would have called 'a funny old codger'. He lived by himself because Mrs Mudge had died, but he had this old dog Flossie. She didn't race round and chase things like Streak does, but it was good to stroke her and let her lick our hands and follow us about.

Mr Mudge's house was rather shabby and could have done with some paint. I suppose I noticed it because all the other houses in the street were so neat and clean. His garden was pretty untidy too, rather like ours at the farm, with weeds in among the flowers, and dirt paths instead of concrete, and some big trees.

We found Mr Mudge in the back garden digging up potatoes. We grew spuds at home sometimes when it wasn't too dry, and I always liked digging them up. It was fun to see what the fork would heave up from under the dirt, sort of like buried treasure. Rosie watched Mr Mudge for a while and I could tell that she was getting excited too as these great big spuds tumbled out. She kept poking her hand in and trying to grab them.

'Watch out,' growled Mr Mudge, 'or I'll spike yer with the fork! You can grub round for the little ones when I've done.'

He didn't dig up the whole patch, just enough for a few meals. Then he gave Rosie a trowel and said, 'Have a fossick round in the dirt and see if I've missed any.'

I bet Rosie had never been spud-digging before, but it didn't take her long to get the hang of it and soon her hands and knees were black. Every time she spotted a baby spud she'd dive on it with a yelp, and soon she had quite a pile. Flossie sat watching and she wagged her tail whenever Rosie yelped.

When she had sifted every bit of earth Rosie said, 'I think that's all. Look, aren't there a lot!'

Mr Mudge picked a couple of the larger spuds out of her pile and said, 'I can't be bothered with those little ones. You can take 'em home for tea, and here's a bit of mint for the pot.'

'Really?' Rosie was tickled pink. You'd think he'd given her a box of chocolate caramels instead of a few potatoes fresh out of the dirt.

By the time Auntie Beryl came home from the library where she worked, Rosie and I had the spuds all ready scrubbed and waiting in their saucepan with the mint. Uncle Dizz had to inspect them to make sure we'd scrubbed every grain of dirt away. I bet he never thought about spuds usually, or where they come from, but just because we told him about digging them up he had one of his worrying fits about dirt and germs. But even *he* said that the spuds were very tasty when they were cooked and had butter melted over them. Victor didn't say anything much, but he polished his plate all right.

Rosie and I went to see Mr Mudge and Flossie almost every day after that. It was hard to tell if he liked our visits or not, but he probably did as he must have been lonely. Flossie was always pleased to see us, you could tell by her tail. Mr Mudge was usually in his garden doing something we could watch or help him with, like picking beans. I dug over a whole bed for him one day, because of his arthritis, and the same day he told Rosie to pick a big bunch of flowers to take to Auntie Beryl. Often the garden was full of butterflies. They flickered among the flowers and weeds, and Rosie and I stalked them and found seven different sorts. Mr Mudge was always complaining about the white cabbage moths, so we hunted for their caterpillars on the turnip tops and cabbages and squashed them to green squelch. Another time Mr Mudge asked me if I could climb the old plum tree and take off some dead bits. Rosie climbed up with me and we could see right over to the park where Victor ran his marathons.

'I wish we had a big tree like this at home,' sighed Rosie.

'My mum said that your dad cut two down when you were little so that you and Victor wouldn't climb them and have an accident. Is that really true?' I asked.

Rosie stared at me. 'Did she say *that*? Nobody ever told *me* and I can't remember it happening, but ... there *are* two stumps in the back yard, aren't there!'

I'd noticed them too. I was just wondering what to say next when Rosie had another of her outbursts, up there in Mr Mudge's plum tree.

'Dad's *hopeless*! He's *nuts*! We could have had two big trees to climb or sit under in our own garden, and he has to go and cut them down! Why does he *do* things like that?'

I was beginning to wish I hadn't told her about Uncle Dizz and his axe, when suddenly she scrambled down to the ground and rushed at Mr Mudge. 'Do you remember if there were two trees at our place once and if Dad chopped them down?' she asked him.

Mr Mudge straightened his creaky back and thought for a bit. 'Yairs, I remember 'em, when you were just a baby. Your dad got a tree-feller in though, didn't do it himself.'

'Do you know *why*? Were the trees dead or something?'

'No fear—decent trees they were. Nothing wrong with 'em. It was a real shame, we all said so, and they would've been a good size by now. Once you've cut 'em down, you can't put 'em back, can you? Dunno why he did it. He said they were dangerous, but no-one else thought so.'

Rosie climbed slowly back into the plum tree. She was a pretty good climber, so she must have learnt to do it at school or somewhere in spite of Uncle Dizz. I went on sawing off dead twigs.

After a while she said, 'Why do you think Dad does things like that?'

It was hard to know what to say. 'Well,' I mumbled, 'I've noticed that he always seems to be scared of what *might* happen, you know, like leaving for work early just in case the trains are on strike, so I suppose he was scared that you'd fall out of the trees or that they'd drop a branch on the house, or something. I guess some people are just like that.'

'Well, I wish he wasn't. He's not much fun. And neither is Victor,' she grumbled.

I didn't like to agree out loud that Victor was a pain, but I did ask her why he was always so busy doing all these extra courses and things. 'Do you think he *likes* doing them?' I said.

'Well, he doesn't like it when things go wrong,' Rosie told me. 'If he doesn't get an A for his tests and assignments he goes bananas! He even *cried* last year when he only got a B-plus for his bassoon exam.'

'*Cried*! Why? Was your dad wild with him?'

'Not exactly wild, just upset. I suppose he realised that Victor wasn't going to be a world famous bassoon player, after all. I could have told him *that*. Anyway, everyone was gloomy for days afterwards.'

Well, I thought, maybe Victor *had* caught the Slingsby disease, but it only showed up when things went wrong, if you could call a B-plus going wrong! I'm always pretty pleased if I even get a B. I suppose Victor was scared he wasn't going to make it and be a big success, and he thought he could only make it by being top all the time. No wonder he wasn't much fun. And another thing about him, he just seemed to be tied up inside himself. At least Uncle Dizz worried about other people as well.

When I'd finished tidying up the plum tree, Rosie and I climbed down. Mr Mudge was among the flowerbeds.

'Come over here a tick.' He pointed. 'Look. There's a decent sort of a butterfly for you!'

It was sitting on a yellow flower, with its wings all spread out.

'Gee, it's a Wanderer!' I said. I'd seen a few before in the country, but this was a beauty.

Rosie was gazing at it, getting as close as she could. 'Wow, it's gorgeous!' she whispered. 'It looks like a leadlight window, all orange and black, with a sort of black-and-white border.' She was quite good at describing things, was Rosie.

The Wanderer sat there in the sun and then it flew off to another flower, quite slowly. It didn't rush about madly like other butterflies, but floated in a lazy sort of way.

'Haven't seen one in years,' said Mr Mudge, stroking Flossie's neck. 'You never know what'll turn up next.' He looked quite pleased.

The Wanderer floated over the fence. 'Will it come back?' wailed Rosie.

'I reckon so,' said Mr Mudge. 'This'll be the sort of garden it likes.'

Rosie was quite excited about butterflies by then. It rained that afternoon, so we decided to go to Auntie Beryl's library to see what we could find out about Wanderers. There were several butterfly books and we found out that this butterfly used to live only in one bit of South America, but now it has spread nearly all over the world.

'I suppose that's why it's called the Wanderer,' I whispered to Rosie. It was a very quiet library.

'Yes, but look—sometimes it's called the Monarch,' she whispered back. 'That name suits it too. It's like the king of Mr Mudge's garden.'

One book said the Wanderer didn't even get to Australia until about 1870. We looked at a map of the world and decided that it couldn't have flown across the Pacific Ocean all by itself, so perhaps it had stowed away on a ship and then laid some eggs when it arrived. Or maybe a chrysalis or two had been on board ship in a bale of straw and had hatched out when they got here. We decided it would be much easier to migrate nowadays, because the Wanderer could catch a jumbo jet. We had a fit of rather snorty giggles thinking about this butterfly queuing up at the airport, with its suitcase and passport, and we had to go outside because people at the next table were shushing us.

We told Uncle Dizz about the Wanderer that night and he seemed quite pleased, but mainly about us going to the library, I think, not about the butterfly. We asked Victor if he'd like to come over to Mr Mudge's next day to see it, but he said he wasn't into butterflies and had more important things lined up. Auntie Beryl said she'd come on the weekend when she had some time, but that was a few days away and I wasn't sure if the Wanderer would still be there. But at least she seemed interested. She *is* Mum's sister, after all.

'Mr Mudge has some terrific trees in his garden,' I said. 'I pruned the old plum today, just took off the dead bits, and it looks much better.' Then I did something cool. 'Your garden would look really good with some proper trees out the back,' I said to the Slingsbys. Rosie's eyes nearly popped.

I could hear Uncle Dizz snorting behind his newspaper and I made faces at Rosie to shut her up, in case she had another outburst. Victor had gone to do his Indonesian homework.

Uncle Dizz then started to tell us what was wrong with trees—you know, their roots got into the drains and cracked the foundations, their branches fell on power lines and the roof, their leaves messed up the paths and blocked the gutters, their trunks fell over and squashed people, and they dropped things on your head and all that stuff. Trees were the Number One Enemy for Uncle Dizz.

I could tell Rosie was getting mad, so I quickly butted in and said that none of these things would happen if you put the tree in the right place and didn't plant something stupid like a river red gum in a city garden. 'There are plenty of smaller trees,' I said. 'My mum's favourites are walnut trees—the only trouble is that they grow rather slowly.'

'Well, there you are, what's the point?' gloomed Uncle Dizz. 'We'd all be dead long before they grew to any size. It'd just be a waste of time and effort.'

That's when Rosie blew up again. 'If everybody said *that*, there wouldn't be any trees in our parks and gardens at all, would there Dad! *Someone's* got to plant them!'

Suddenly Auntie Beryl interrupted. 'I think an apple tree would be nice, and perhaps a lemon too. Growing a bit of our own fruit would be quite exciting, and they're only smallish trees, not a bit dangerous.' What a turn up! Good old Auntie Beryl!

Uncle Dizz got up then, grumbling about pruning and codling moths and collar rot and all the fruit tree diseases he could think of, and went off to his study to worry about his superannuation or something.

Rosie was grinning at me now, so I thought that while we had Auntie Beryl all fired up we'd better hurry things along. 'If you can get the trees while I'm here, I'll help you to plant them,' I offered. I knew how to do it because I sometimes helped Dad to plant trees for windbreaks and bird shelters and things.

So Auntie Beryl agreed that we could go to a nursery the next Saturday, and we did, just the three of us. Victor was at his golf clinic and Uncle Dizz was at the other clinic for his monthly medical checkup. It was amazing that he didn't have about fifteen stomach ulcers already.

It was a good nursery and Auntie Beryl chose quite a big lemon tree and a Granny Smith apple, and then Rosie and I talked her into buying a jacaranda as well, because of its flowers and feathery leaves. That afternoon we carefully chose the best places for them in the garden and put them in.

Just as well, because soon after that I went back to the farm. Dad's leg was mending and he was allowed to go home. He needed me to help Mum with all the jobs he still couldn't do round the place, and we were flat out catching up with everything. Streak almost knocked me unconscious when I got home, he was so excited, and I was pretty pleased to see him too.

Of course Mum and Dad wanted to know all about the Slingsbys and what I'd done while I was there, but there wasn't much to tell really—you know, it was just mucking about and visiting Mr Mudge, and almost doing a school holiday programme but not quite. Holidays in the city are supposed to be full of excitement and trips to museums and shops and cinemas, but staying with the Slingsbys wasn't like that.

The funny thing was that I had quite enjoyed my visit, when I thought about it. I hadn't been looking forward to going much and it was boring some of the time, but there had been some surprises. I'd thought Victor would have been the one I'd make friends with, but it turned out to be Rosie. And then Auntie Beryl had suddenly been on our side about the trees, and now there were three new trees instead of Uncle Dizz's old stumps. And it was fun remembering things like the spuds and the Wanderer, and getting the giggles in the library and Rosie's outbursts. I suppose they were only small things, but they were all surprises. I remembered Mr Mudge saying, 'You never know what'll turn up next.' I wondered if Victor had room for any surprises in his timetable. He hadn't had a spare minute for the Wanderer. I hoped Auntie Beryl had been able to go and see it by now, anyway.

131

'Tell us about old Dizz,' said Dad. 'Is he as dismal as ever?'

'He's pretty bad,' I said and told them about some of his glooms, right up to the lemon tree dying of collar rot.

'Poor old Mal never thinks that something *good* might happen,' sighed Mum. 'You know, put a lemon tree in front of him and he thinks of collar rot. *I* think of jugs of iced lemon squash.'

Dad said he thought of bees in the blossom, and I straight away thought of lemon meringue pie.

Then Mum asked me if I'd like to invite Rosie to come to the farm for the next holidays.

Well of course I said yes, and I told them that Rosie wanted to meet Streak because Uncle Dizz wouldn't let her have a dog.

'In case all the Slingsbys get rabies, I suppose,' grinned Dad. 'Well, we ought to have some new puppies by then.'

I told Mum not to mention things like animals and big trees and the dam where the wild ducks come when she wrote to the Slingsbys, in case Uncle Dizz started worrying about all the disasters that could happen to Rosie and wouldn't let her visit us. Auntie Beryl must have worked on him, because Rosie *is* coming next holidays and now I'm looking forward to all the things we'll be able to do. And this time I'll tell her about giving the kiss of life to the calf—I might even show her how to do it herself if we can find another groggy calf. I reckon Rosie is about ready for that now.

New Brooms

Mrs Bravo saw the advertisement in the local paper as she gulped her breakfast coffee.

Is Your Home a
PIGSTY?
Call BETTINA SPARKLE,
Domestic Planning
Counsellor

Over the coffee cup, Mrs Bravo surveyed her personal pigsty. Well, there was no actual mud or pig swill in view so perhaps 'bomb site' or 'local tip' were more suitable descriptions for the scene around her. Dishevelled magazines and newspapers littered the floors; smeary glasses and coffee-stained mugs sat abandoned on shelves and window sills; flowers wilted in vases; a scattering of balls, jogging shoes and a skateboard across the floors made walking perilous. She knew without looking that every bedroom would be ankle deep in flung-off clothing and that none of the beds would be made. There was a musty smell of stale pizza and dogs. And now she had to rush off to work, so the bomb site would still be there when everyone arrived home later in the day.

With a shriek of despair, Mrs Bravo grabbed the local paper and fled, slamming the door behind her.

Bettina Sparkle in person took Mrs Bravo's lunchtime phone call. Mrs Bravo had spent the morning's spare moments convincing herself that she needed advice and nerving herself to make the call, but when she finally dialled the number and heard Ms Sparkle's cool efficient tones, all she could say was, 'I think I need *HELP*!' Ms Sparkle, Domestic Planning Counsellor, lost no time in coming to her aid, and after a few probing questions she began to enter the Bravo Household Profile into her computer file:

```
Name: BRAVO
Wife: Cheryl (40). Recently returned to
full-time employment. Receptionist.
Husband: Raymond (43). Local Government
Officer.
Children: Harvey (M 14), Phoebe (F 11)
Sidney (M 7). At school.
Pets: 2 dogs, 3 goldfish.
```

'Now, what I need to do,' she told Mrs Bravo, 'is to carry out an on-site assessment of your problems.'

Panic enveloped Mrs Bravo. 'You mean ... visit me at home?' she squeaked. An image of unmade beds and dirty mugs whirled through her mind.

Bettina Sparkle was firm. 'Yes, on site. Don't panic about the mess,' she said sternly. 'I am professionally detached. I need to see the house in its negative state, so you are not to attempt to tidy up. And,' she added, 'I need to interview the whole family. They are a part of the equation.'

She made it sound like a maths problem, which in fact it was. As Mrs Bravo herself often said, there were just not enough hours in her day.

'Can you all be here tomorrow at about 5.30?' Mrs Bravo asked the family that night. 'I want you to meet someone—she's coming to discuss the housework.' Mrs Bravo avoided the word 'interview'.

'Are we getting a cleaning lady?' asked Phoebe who was lying on the floor consulting the television programmes.

'Well, I'm thinking about it,' said her mother, evasively.

'Why do *I* have to meet her?' growled Harvey. 'That sort of stuff isn't my scene.'

'I know, Harvey, I'm well aware of that—but she specially asked to meet you all. Her name is Bettina Sparkle.'

'She sounds like a fairy godmother!' said Sidney.

'Let's hope she can wave a magic wand,' floated the voice of Mr Bravo from behind the evening paper. 'Can we afford her?'

'I'll pay,' said his wife, grimly. 'I'm a working woman now, remember?'

The family assembled unwillingly in the living room late next day. They sighed and flopped about.

'You usually tidy up a bit when somebody's coming,' Phoebe remarked to her mother.

'Not this time—Ms Sparkle wants to see what she's in for.'

135

'You mean ... she's going to check *us* out? I thought we were checking *her*!'

Before Mrs Bravo could reply, the doorbell rang loudly, twice. Something about that imperious ring caused Mr Bravo to peer over his newspaper and the children to sit up a little straighter while Mrs Bravo went to answer it. Each of them had a private vision of the cleaning lady who was about to appear before them—someone in an overall and flat, practical shoes, carrying a bucket, dusters and mops. In Sidney's vision she also carried a magic wand.

They were all wrong.

'Good evening, Mrs Bravo!' The confident voice rolled from the hallway into the living room, followed by the arresting figure of Ms Bettina Sparkle herself— a stylish blend of navy blue suit, elegant high-heeled shoes and perfect legs, hair alive with auburn tints, gold earrings, a richly patterned silk scarf caught by a gold pin-brooch, a sleek leather briefcase and an aura of tantalising perfume. Not a mop or a bucket in sight.

A blush flooded across Harvey's cheeks as he stared at her.

Sidney eyed the gold pin-brooch. Could it be a computerised magic wand?

Mr Bravo's newspaper fell to the floor to add to the litter, as he rose to his slipper-clad feet and stammered, 'G ... good evening.'

'Good evening Mr Bravo. Please sit,' ordered Ms Sparkle, 'while I do my preliminary on-site assessment. Take me through it, Mrs Bravo.' The family sat, paralysed.

Meekly Mrs Bravo led the way through the bomb site. Ms Sparkle glanced mercilessly into bedrooms, inspected the shower recess and the bathroom floor at rather more length, jerked open kitchen cupboards and deftly caught whatever fell out, and gave the oven a long hard look. She sized up the piles of ironing in the laundry and estimated the thickness of frost in the freezer and of dust on the bookshelves. The dogs had been shut outside, but she ordered them in to assess their moult and dribble problems, and she sniffed the goldfish bowl for signs of algae. She then led the way back to the living room.

The family had been whispering together, but they now sat up stiffly to hear the judge pass sentence. Ms Sparkle drew out a clipboard from her briefcase and snapped a gold ballpoint pen into action. She entered several mysterious symbols on a form, but she gave no indication of whether the Bravo household had passed or failed the test.

'Now,' she said. 'I have some questions for all the family. The answers will provide me with a useful profile of your domestic attitudes.'

Sidney's brow crumpled but he didn't dare to ask what she meant. Phoebe felt internal twinges like exam nerves.

'Question One,' announced Ms Sparkle. 'Who generally cleans the bathroom and toilet in this house?'

Mrs Bravo cleared her throat. 'I do—always,' she said nervously, wondering about the mould level. No-one else spoke. Bettina Sparkle jotted more symbols on the form.

'I see,' she said after a pause. 'Now, let me ask each of you others why you *don't* clean the bathroom and toilet? I take it that you all *use* them?'

'That cleaning stuff's not *my* job,' blurted the blushing Harvey. 'Cleaning and stuff's boring.'

Mr Bravo was about to say that it wasn't his job either, but he noted a steely glint in Ms Sparkle's eye and he changed his approach. 'My wife does it so much better than I ever could.' He smiled tenderly at Mrs Bravo, who didn't smile back.

Phoebe said gruffly she didn't have time for cleaning because of her homework load. Sidney explained that he didn't know the bathroom and toilet needed cleaning. He thought they cleaned themselves when the shower or the cistern came on.

'I see,' said Ms Sparkle, jotting some more. 'Question Two now. From the following items I want you to select the one you consider most important to your well-being: *(a)* Freshly ironed shirts; *(b)* a well-stocked refrigerator; *(c)* a tidy bedroom; *(d)* a germ-free toilet.'

The children all chose the food. Mr Bravo, who liked to leave very early for work, decided on the shirts, and Mrs Bravo had no hesitation in choosing the germ-free toilet.

'Hey, Mum! Why did you choose that?' cried Harvey. 'Why not the full fridge? Wouldn't you *care* if we all starved?'

'Starved? You don't know the meaning of the word! And I'd rather have a slightly hungry family than a gastro epidemic, any time,' sniffed his mother, who had endured one or two of the latter.

This time Mr Bravo thought he detected a gleam of approval in Ms Sparkle's expression, so he said, rather crossly, 'Where is all this leading to, anyway? Are you prepared to come and clean our house for us, or not?'

Mrs Bravo shut her eyes in horror, but Ms Sparkle merely shook her head and said, briskly, 'Goodness me, no. You don't understand my position Mr Bravo— *I* don't clean houses. I am a Domestic Planning Counsellor and I am here to devise a programme which will enable you to clean your own house. All of you,' she added.

'*All* of us?' gaped Phoebe. 'It's always been Mum's job!'

'D'you mean me?' stared Sidney.

'Now, look here ...' began Mr Bravo.

'Will we get paid?' asked Harvey.

Ms Sparkle fixed her eye on Harvey. 'Your mother never has, I take it, so why should you? The rewards for domestic efficiency, young man, are a hygienic and comfortable home to live in, health and good grooming. All of those things are your payment.'

'Well, yuk,' said Harvey, who was allergic to grooming. But he blushed again.

Ignoring him, Ms Sparkle drew several colour-coded charts from her briefcase. 'Now, what I have here is the Sparkle System of Household Management which allocates different duties to each member of the team on a weekly rotation plan. I must emphasise the teamwork ethic here—a team is only as strong as its weakest member, as you young persons will know from the sporting field.'

The young persons were sitting like stones.

'For example, now,' Ms Sparkle went on, 'this pink form covers all tasks related to House Hygiene—cleaning the bathroom, washing the dogs, collecting and sorting the garbage and putting it out for collection, aerating the goldfish, etc. Anyone in the Bravo family can do these jobs, regardless of age.'

At least four of the Bravo family looked unconvinced.

Next Ms Sparkle selected a yellow chart. 'There are, however, certain duties which are largely the responsibility of adults, such as the weekly shopping—because this usually involves driving the car and large sums of money. Nevertheless, one young person should be rostered to assist each week with trolley-pushing, bag-carrying and unpacking, and everyone can help to compile the weekly list of items.'

Ms Sparkle explained the other charts—cooking, laundry, floors, outside jobs, etc.—and she insisted that bedrooms were the personal responsibility of each occupant. This meant bed-making, tidying and dusting, and conveying one's own soiled clothes to the laundry basket.

'It's up to each of you whether or not you choose to inhabit a bedroom slum, although I should warn you of the health risks of dust mites, fleas and stale food scraps.'

Mrs Bravo winced.

Winding up, Ms Sparkle said, 'There is one rule that must never be broken, except in cases of emergency or illness. You are not on any account to do someone else's jobs. If one person fails to do the ironing or to put out the rubbish, the rest of you have to live with that. This rule will be particularly hard for *you* to obey, Mrs Bravo, as you are so conditioned to covering for other people, but you really must let them sink or swim.'

'Yes, I suppose so,' said Mrs Bravo weakly, expecting them all to sink.

'Now,' concluded Bettina Sparkle, Domestic Planning Counsellor, 'I'll leave these forms with you to fill out for yourselves, after you have negotiated the various duties for the week, and I shall return in a month's time to assess your progress.'

The next week was peppery. Mrs Bravo didn't feel that she'd been counselled—rolled flat, more like, but she couldn't admit that to the family.

Mr Bravo constantly referred to Bettina Sparkle as 'that interfering woman'.

'Why did you bring *her* into it? Why couldn't you ask us yourself, if you need help?' he flared at his wife.

140

'As long as I have to ask five or six times, it's called nagging, and anyway nothing much ever happens when I *do* ask,' replied Mrs Bravo, with spirit. 'So I thought I'd bring in a professional, a neutral arbitrator—and let me remind you that I'm paying for her services!'

Trying to arrange the Sparkle System roster so that everyone had jobs to match their abilities was not made any easier by Mr Bravo and the children insisting that they had no housework skills at all.

'Well, you can all learn on the job, like I did. If mere housewives can perform these things, why can't you?' cried Mrs Bravo, who was feeling sarcastic. 'What's so difficult about them?'

'Oh well,' muttered Phoebe, 'I bags aerate the goldfish.'

'Big deal!' scoffed Harvey, wishing he'd thought of that.

Mrs Bravo seized the chance. 'Thank you Phoebe. The goldfish come into the House Hygiene jobs file, so you'll also be responsible for the garbage, washing the dogs and cleaning the bathroom and toilets.'

Phoebe groaned. Harvey smirked.

Mr Bravo sighed, wishing he'd never set eyes on wretched Bettina Sparkle. 'Okay, put me down for the outside jobs, whatever they are,' he said. To Mr Bravo, Outside Jobs seemed far more manly than ironing or vacuuming. When it came to the point, they amounted to little more than mowing the small lawn and sweeping the paths and the verandah, so Mrs Bravo put his name down for the Friday evening shopping as well, assisted by Sidney.

That left Cooking, Laundry and Floors. The wet area floors were transferred to Phoebe and Hygiene, while Sidney was given the carpet vacuuming and general tidying. Harvey was now left with the choice of laundry or cooking dinners.

'Cooking, any time,' he grunted, deciding at once on seven nights of varied takeaways.

Mrs Bravo wondered if the family would survive a full week of Harvey's cooking. However, she had promised Bettina Sparkle to obey the rules, so she said, 'Right, then I'll take Laundry. Harvey, as Cook you'll need to discuss the shopping list with your father before Friday evening. We'll start our new system then.'

Harvey's takeaway meals plan was shot down in flames immediately. 'You'll never learn to cook that way,' said his mother.

'More likely die of heart disease,' added Phoebe.

'If bankruptcy doesn't overtake us first,' said his father.

Mr Bravo returned very cheerful from the first shopping expedition, claiming to have saved at least $75 on the normal weekly bill. He had too, but the food supply and various staple items like toothpaste and detergent ran out two days later and he had to go shopping again.

'It's Harvey's fault,' he snapped. 'His list was full of gaps. How was I to know we needed milk and bread and toothpaste?'

Mrs Bravo said nothing, but felt her blood pressure mounting.

Harvey's culinary skills amounted to two—he could light the oven and he could boil water. His menus therefore alternated between oven-heated frozen pizza and chips, and boiled frankfurts and chips, with lots of tomato sauce to fill in the gaps where the greens should have been. By the fifth night the family were fantasising about broccoli. Mrs Bravo decided to roster herself as cook every second week during this learning-on-the-job stage, so she could introduce some fruit and vegetables to ward off an outbreak of scurvy.

Her own duties in the laundry went perfectly smoothly, and for once she had time to keep up with the ironing. The only hitches were not her fault— Harvey and Sidney both forgot to convey their own dirty clothes to the laundry basket, so they ran out of clean socks and shirts and footie shorts before the end of the week.

'It's no use complaining to me,' she told them, obeying the Sparkle System rules. 'You forgot and you have to live with it. And it's not my fault that you have to wear muddy shorts for the football match, Harvey.'

She also had to wash one of the net curtains which Sidney had tried to vacuum; it had vanished gurgling into the vacuum hose and it took two people to pull it out. Sidney was sternly told to concentrate on the carpets. He wrestled bravely with the vacuum cleaner and chipped five hunks of paint off the doors. He also sucked up Harvey's best ballpoint pen, three of Phoebe's hair scrunchies and several pieces of scrabble, including the letter Q.

Phoebe was quite skilled at goldfish-aerating and dog-washing. Unfortunately, she had to wash the dogs twice that week, because she had forgotten to put the garbage bin out for collection. The garbage stench had ripened during the week until the frantic dogs tore the lid off the bin, scratched the contents all over the yard and rolled in the smelliest bits. Mr Bravo (on Outside Jobs) was enraged when he saw the mess. He said it could jolly well wait.

'Phoebe can be on Outside Jobs next week and clean it up,' he fumed. 'It's all her fault for forgetting the bin.'

By the end of the first week, the state of the Bravo bomb site was, if anything, worse, and the family tempers were badly frayed. Mrs Bravo had had more time to herself than she had ever known before, but she spent most of it worrying about scurvy, rats, dust mites and what Bettina Sparkle was going to say when she paid her next visit in three weeks' time.

In Week Two, Mr Bravo took over Laundry Duties. He supposed it wasn't too unmanly to switch on the power and push a few buttons—rather like operating a computer, really. And once the machine was going, he could walk away and pretend he wasn't responsible for it. The ironing didn't take him long at all. He carefully ironed his own shirt collars and assumed that all the other items in the basket were drip-dry. Sidney again forgot to pick up his dirty clothes. He began to smell and everyone else looked creased.

Harvey, on Hygiene, remembered to put the garbage out. The bin was overflowing after Phoebe had scraped up all the mess in the yard, and everyone's second remark was 'Phhhew!'—so it was hard to forget the garbage. Harvey reckoned that if only the dogs stayed out of the bin he might get away with not washing them (as they'd been done twice the week before). He was so busy working towards putting the garbage out and not washing the dogs that he totally forgot to clean and mop up the bathroom, until people were complaining about that too.

'Soggy towels! Swamp! Bug-pit!' they yelled. 'Get with it, Harvey!'

Back in the kitchen, Mrs Bravo was the star of the week. To her surprise, the family almost fell upon her anti-scurvy salads and steamed vegetables. It was her turn to do the shopping, too. She took Phoebe to help

144

and they restocked with all the things that had been forgotten the week before when Mr Bravo and Sidney had been specialising in soft drinks, chocolate biscuits and Footie bandaids.

Sidney had asked to be on floors and tidying duty again, because vacuuming gave him valuable practice as a Bobcat driver, which was his chosen career in life. He'd learned to leave the net curtains alone and to pick up small items from the carpet before the vacuum cleaner devoured them, and that week there were only three chips in the paintwork instead of five. Sidney was, in fact, the first of the family to show signs of learning on the job.

By the third and fourth weeks, Mrs Bravo thought she could sense a subtle shift in domestic attitudes. Each team member was on the alert for slackness among the others; the competitive edge was growing sharper.

'Sidney forgot his dirty socks *again*. He stinks!'

'Who left that cricket stump on the floor? I nearly busted my ankle!'

'Dad forgot to buy Vegemite—he's so useless!'

'You kids—your schoolbags are repulsive! Look! Chewed crusts, mouldy celery, *more* filthy socks, old tissues, thirteen food wrappers, four squashed drink cans ... talk about scumbags! Take them out and hose them!'

Phoebe, now on Laundry, elaborately ironed everything in sight just to show up her father's miserable efforts at the ironing board the week before. Mr Bravo, who became Cook in Week Four, attempted to restore his damaged image by producing menus of great originality, starting with Cheesy Fish Pie accompanied by Stir-fried Oriental Vegetables in Orange Sauce.

145

'Hey, Dad! We don't believe this!' was the general opinion.

After this unexpected success, Mr Bravo remarked that the world's greatest chefs were mainly men, and Harvey, when he thought no-one was looking, was seen to be reading a recipe book. He slobbered over a coloured photo of a Lemon Meringue Pie. What a knockout! Could he make one of those so that Bettina Sparkle would at last recognise his genius and charm?

Mrs Bravo dared to hope that something like what the newspapers called 'market forces' were at work in her household and creating new standards. Another force was at work, too. On the Thursday of Week Four Bettina Sparkle was due to make her first return inspection.

Mrs Bravo examined the Week Four roster for weak spots. Harvey on Outside Duty couldn't do much harm, surely. Mr Bravo was showing unheard of creative skills as Cook. Phoebe, in the Laundry, was even ironing the socks, whereas Mrs Bravo herself was on Floors and Tidying duty and would certainly do her best to present Ms Sparkle with a gleaming first impression.

The weak spot was likely to be Sidney, who was doing his first round of Hygiene Duty.

Now, Sidney could cope with the goldfish and the dogs. He would happily have washed the dogs every day, given the chance, but his father said they would get eczema. Sidney could manage the garbage, too. It was the bathroom which Mrs Bravo foresaw as his greatest challenge, as he was only seven, and she thought it prudent to give him a little coaching in cleaning tiles and polishing glass as there wasn't much time for him to learn on the job before Ms Sparkle's arrival late on Thursday. After all, Sidney had said that he thought the bathroom cleaned itself.

Mrs Bravo introduced Sidney to the battery of bottles and sprays containing powerful mould destroyer, biodegradable lemon-scented cream cleanser (for fighting grime), household grade disinfectant (for fighting dangerous bacteria), steam-barrier formula glass cleaner, and concentrated air freshener (jasmine scented). It occurred to her to make him wear protective goggles, so that learning on the job didn't include an eyeful of powerful mould destroyer. She showed him which sponges and mops and brushes to use and how to shine the taps and polish the mirror and rub the grime off the basin and the shower screen.

After his mother had left him to it, Sidney donned his goggles and grabbed two powerful spray cans. He could easily imagine himself into a Star Wars role, fighting bacteria on all fronts, but he was apt to polish the taps with disinfectant, scrub the toilet with air freshener and spray the air with the mould destroyer. It didn't seem to matter—they all had much the same effect. His worst problem was removing his own muddy footprints after he'd been in the bath and the shower recess fighting the war against grime.

Thursday arrived. After school Phoebe put the finishing touches to her immaculate laundry. The dirty clothes basket was empty. The rail was filled with freshly ironed shirts and skirts and the rest of the ironing was neatly folded and stacked in piles. Harvey gave the front verandah a quick swish with the broom and then went and did his hair, spending ten minutes at the mirror. Mrs Bravo put away the vacuum after a last dash over the carpets.

Mr Bravo had left work spot on five o'clock so as to

be well ahead in his dinner preparations when Ms Sparkle arrived. He donned his striped apron and opened the recipe book to Italian Meatball Casserole.

'I'll show her, that Sparkle dame,' he muttered, sharpening his knife. 'I'll show her.'

Harvey, with his hair carefully combed back, was casually studying a cookery book on his newly-swept front verandah when Bettina Sparkle arrived, so she had no need to ring the bell. Harvey, his cheeks glowing, jumped up to open the door, saying gruffly, 'Um ... come in, please.' A gust of perfume left him reeling as she passed.

The rest of the family was waiting nervously in the unnaturally tidy living room, except for Mr Bravo who went on frying onions in the kitchen. He had decided not to notice her arrival.

Bettina Sparkle drew out her clipboard and her gold ballpoint and began the round of inspection. She maintained her professional detachment as she noted the tidy floors, the gleaming mirrors, the neat piles of clean laundry, the delicious aroma from the kitchen, the fluffy dogs. She made no comment until she'd finished her rounds. By that time, the Bravos were stiff with apprehension.

'I like what I see!' cried Ms Sparkle. 'This is most satisfactory progress—the house is a fine testimony to the Sparkle System and it just shows what a little teamwork and method can achieve.' The family sagged with relief. 'I have only two minor criticisms,' she went on.

Mrs Bravo's pride ebbed away. 'Oh,' she cried, 'what are they?'

'Well, firstly—I think the bathroom could do with

considerably less mould destroyer. The air in there is somewhat lethal. And secondly, I have to tell you there is a large toad in the shower recess.'

'What!' gasped Mrs Bravo. 'There can't be!'

'Yes there is—it's Bernard,' said Sidney. 'He's mine.' Everyone glared at him, speechless.

'He wasn't entered on the list of household pets, was he?' demanded Ms Sparkle.

'No, I've only just got him—at school today,' said Sidney. 'I swapped a whole set of Batman cards for him, and I thought he'd like to be in the nice germ-free shower recess just until he's got used to us. He'll probably fret for a while. I hope you closed the door—he's very valuable.'

'Certainly I did,' replied Ms Sparkle, whose professional front was wilting slightly. Eventually she snapped off her gold ballpoint and said, 'Well, I'll overlook Bernard this time, but I hope that he will have more suitable accommodation long before I make my final assessment in six weeks time.'

'You bet he will,' interrupted Mr Bravo. 'I'm not sharing my shower with any toad, even if he is fretting.' He rather hoped that mould destroyer worked on toads as well as fungus.

'Quite,' said Ms Sparkle, and this time Mr Bravo believed that her gleam of approval was directed at him.

Bernard the toad preyed on Mrs Bravo's mind all the next day. How could Sidney have spoiled things like that? She hoped that Ms Sparkle understood small boys. She found herself wondering about Bettina Sparkle's own house. It would be spotless, of course. If she had a family they would have been trained from birth in the Sparkle System.

After work, on impulse, Mrs Bravo bought a spectacular bunch of flowers from a florist's stall and scribbled on a card—

To Ms Bettina Sparkle—Grateful thanks for getting my life together and many apologies for 'Bernard'.
Best wishes, Cheryl Bravo

Ms Sparkle's office wasn't far away. She'd drop the flowers in as she passed and Ms Sparkle would have the weekend to enjoy them and to forget the dreadful toad.

Ms Sparkle's receptionist was tidying up before closing for the weekend. 'What beautiful flowers!' she cried, as Mrs Bravo entered.

'They're for Ms Sparkle. Can I leave them for her?'

'Oh dear—what a *shame*! Ms Sparkle has already gone. She had one more inspection to make on her way home.'

Mrs Bravo felt foolish. 'Never mind—it was silly of me to rush in like this on a Friday. I should have thought ... but I just wanted her to have these ... er ... on behalf of my small son, really.'

'That is a *shame*,' repeated the receptionist, who was closing drawers and locking cupboards. 'Look, I know—I'll just ring her home number and see if she's back ... perhaps I could drop them in on my way past.'

As she dialled the number, the door opened and another late customer flew in.

The receptionist waved the phone at Mrs Bravo. 'I've dialled through—perhaps you could sort something out while I attend to this client? Things are a bit rushed at this time of day.'

Nervously Mrs Bravo took the phone just in time to

hear a man's deep voice say, 'Good afternoon—the Sparkle residence.'

'I'm sorry to bother you,' stammered Mrs Bravo. 'Could I possibly speak to Ms Sparkle?'

'Not at the moment, I'm afraid. She has not yet returned.'

'Oh, I see.' Mrs Bravo swallowed. She felt embarrassed. 'Er ... is that Mr Sparkle speaking?'

'Oh no, Madam,' said the voice. 'This is Dustin. I am Ms Sparkle's housekeeper.'

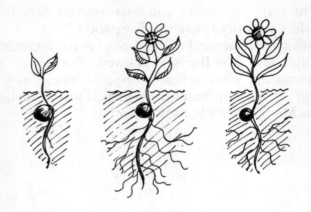

Afterword:
Having an Idea

Writers are often asked 'Where do you get your ideas from?', as though they have some special secret storehouse or supermarket which they raid whenever a story is required.

There is no real mystery about it; the ideas are out there in the world, in conversations, in newspapers and books, in daily events; or they are buried in one's own memory bank of past experiences. But there has to be a flash, a moment of recognition (sometimes called 'inspiration'), when the writer seizes some small idea as the starting point for a story. Or maybe the idea seizes the writer.

To put it another way, the idea is like a seed. A seed has the potential to develop into something like a gum tree or a rose bush or a watermelon, but it cannot do this unless it is planted in fertile soil and then fed and watered and pruned as it grows. So with a story—it often starts with a very simple 'seed' of an idea. The writer plants this in the fertile soil of imagination and gradually the seed puts out roots and shoots, then branches and leaves, as the plot and the characters and the setting of the story develop. (It doesn't always happen of course—sometimes the seed is a dud!)

Quite often (in my case anyway) the early stages of a story don't involve much writing at all. Like a seed underground in the dark, the idea is hidden away in the mind and in the imagination for some time (weeks or months even) before it begins to show itself, but by then it has some strong roots and promising shoots. This is when the writing begins—sketches, plans and rough drafts at first, research and fact-checking, then gradually more detail, and usually some pruning into shape towards the end.

The stories in this book all began from simple ideas. Some of the ideas came to me in a flash, some drifted more gently to the surface from deep in my memory, and for others I had to think hard to find a starting point. This is how each of these stories began.

A Bit of a Hitch

When I visit schools, I am sometimes asked to explain how a small idea can be turned into a story. One of the most important ingredients in a story is suspense—the reader wants to know what is going to happen. If you want the reader to keep reading, it is important not to let everything in the story happen at once or too soon!

To illustrate this, I tried to think of some simple starting points for a story which would lead to a build-up of suspense. After a while, something floated to the surface of my memory. Eggs hatching! Chooks were always a part of my childhood and hatching chickens under a broody hen was a common but exciting occurrence. Suspense is certainly built into the hatching process because Nature can't be hurried. Hens' eggs take three weeks to hatch and as a child I found those weeks an unbearably long time to wait. What would we find under the hen on the twenty-first day? Healthy, fluffy chicks? Squashed chicks? Addled eggs?

To substitute crocodiles for chooks, and therefore increase the waiting time from weeks to months, would mean a real recipe for suspense, I decided.

So I presented different groups of school children with a few facts to start off a story; an uncle or an older brother comes home with some crocodile eggs and asks the younger children to mind them for a few days. Crocodiles are a protected species, so the children are sworn to secrecy. From this simple start, I asked the school children to work out a story line. What would happen if ...?

There were various suggestions from the school groups I talked to, but almost all of them began their stories by having the eggs hatch out immediately on the first or second page, followed by Mum having hysterics and Dad ringing the police. Crocodiles galore! No-one considered the importance of suspense, and very few thought that some research into crocodiles might be helpful.

To demonstrate what I meant, I decided to finish the story myself, as I saw it, and the characters gradually evolved.

The Crossing
There is a pedestrian crossing near where I live, near

the bottom of a dip on a very busy road. I know of at least one person who was killed on that crossing, so when I use it I am a bit nervous because the cars and trucks gather speed as they come down the hill. It is always reassuring when the crossing supervisor is on duty with his lollipop and his whistle.

That background plus another incident led to this story. When my children had left home, we decided to give away the budgies and finches in our aviary. I asked the mother of a young family if she knew of a good home for the birds and she immediately said, 'I'll ask the school crossing lady. She'll know someone.' She did, too. Within a couple of days a beaming small boy and his mother arrived with a cage to collect the birds.

This made me realise that school crossings are a sort of modern equivalent of the fords or ferries or bridges across streams in former times, a place where you'd often meet familiar people and exchange news and information. Now, in our cities and suburbs, we have torrents of traffic to negotiate instead of unbridged rivers.

If you want to find out more about Moses and the crossing of the Red Sea, you can find it in Chapter 14 of Exodus in the Old Testament of the Bible.

Lulu

This was another idea which had been stored in my memory and it floated to the surface—perhaps while I was thinking of eggs hatching ('A Bit of a Hitch'). Some years ago a young neighbour, Dianne, brought home a day-old chicken from school to study the 'bonding' process. Dianne wanted to keep the chick for as long as possible in her bedroom, and she asked me if I'd be willing to give it a home later on with my bantam chooks in the back garden. I agreed, of course.

The chicken became three chickens during the next few weeks as Dianne adopted others from her schoolmates, and all three came to live with me. Two of them turned out to be very boisterous roosters and they were sent to the country. Dianne's own chicken grew into a lovely Light Sussex hen, big, fluffy and friendly, and we all loved her dearly.

There are many blocks of villa units and flats in my suburb and I have heard various tales about the rules of the 'Body Corporate' regarding pets. It didn't take long for the villa unit idea to attach itself to the day-old chicken idea, and the human characters then began to develop.

Aunt Millicent

This story and 'Staying with the Slingsbys' are a bit different from the others because they were both 'written to order'.

The Children's Book Council of Australia decided to publish an anthology of stories by Australian children's writers, and they invited a number of us to contribute. The title of the book was to be *Dream Time* and we were asked to use that theme to start us off.

I thought hard for a couple of months about different sorts of dreaming—nightmares, fantasy, aboriginal legends, etc., and finally I chose the idea of day-dreaming and imagining. I remembered how very young children often invent characters, and talk and play with them. My own children invented a whole rowdy family of two parents and fifteen kids who 'lived' with us for several years.

As children grow up they tend to stop doing this sort of thing, which I think is rather a pity, so I helped Jamie Nutbeam and his family to invent or 'dream up'

Aunt Millicent. After all, this is what fiction writers do all the time.

My Bonnie Lies Over the Ocean

This tale owes its existence to a particular incident, but I didn't write the story until some years after the event.

Our telephone rang one evening, and when my husband answered it a very Scottish voice said, 'Halloo, wheer are you?'

My husband said, 'In Melbourne.'

'Wheer? Wheer's that?'

'Melbourne, in Australia.'

'*Austreeliya*!'

'Yes, Australia! Where are you calling from?'

'From Scotland!'

'*Really*? Well - who do you want?'

'Och—I'm jist wanting to say halloo to someone—anyone'll du! You'll du!'

This Scotsman was much older than Fergus McPhee and obviously he had taken a good dose of his national drink, but it was a comic incident which I filed away in my memory and eventually it became the seed for this story.

Bate

This was one of the 'sudden flash' ideas. It came to me when I was walking to the local shopping centre one day. The sun was shining and I hummed a tune as I walked past the computer shop, the aerobics centre, the dry cleaner's, the dental clinic, the petrol station, the traffic lights and all the cars and trucks using the busy road.

I suddenly realised that the tune I hummed was by Ludwig van Beethoven. He wrote it nearly 200 years ago on the other side of the world, yet here I was absent-mindedly humming it in an Australian suburban street in the 1990s. If Beethoven himself had been dropped into this street, he would have been mystified by what he saw, even terrified, yet here was his tune taking part in it all.

The idea began to grow roots. As I walked home, I remembered other incidents. Two years earlier, I'd been flying to London in a Jumbo jet. Somewhere over Russia, in the blackest night, with a few tiny twinkly lights miles below, I put on the headset and listened to some music by J.S.Bach. It was weird—up there, sealed in that Boeing 747, I could listen to Bach's music nearly 300 years after he composed it. What would he have thought if he'd been sitting beside me?

Then I remembered being about fourteen and hearing Beethoven's 5th Piano Concerto ('The Emperor') for the first time. It was a direct, rather crackly radio broadcast from the Melbourne Town Hall with Hephzibah Menuhin as the soloist. The Second World War was just over and this concert was something of a celebration. LP recordings were not yet available, so we'd not had many opportunities to hear such performances. Next day at school an old teacher said with tears in her eyes, 'How wonderful to hear such music again.' I knew that I had heard something special.

By now, the little seed idea was beginning to grow quite big branches as I thought about history and music and the technology which made it possible to listen to Bach (or Beethoven or ABBA) in a Jumbo jet. That technology included those old composers writing their musical scores down on paper with their scratchy quill pens, as well as the wind-up gramophones and the crackly radio of my childhood and the

CDs and cassette players of today. Only fifty or sixty years ago, we didn't know about television, computers, faxes, ballpoint pens, plastic, organ transplants, jet aircraft, antibiotics ... hosts of things which nowadays we (and especially young people) take for granted.

Staying with the Slingsbys

Like 'Aunt Millicent', this story was written to order for one of the Children's Book Council's anthologies. The title and theme of this book was *Into the Future*.

Once again I thought for some time about possible ways of interpreting the theme, such as space travel or science fiction, but I wasn't very confident about writing that sort of story. I realised that the future doesn't just mean the twenty-first century and beyond; the future starts from *now* and includes the next half hour and tomorrow and next week. So I began to think about people's *attitudes* to the future and to life. These attitudes can be broadly divided between the optimistic ('No worries—she'll be right!') and the pessimistic ('Do be careful!' 'What's to become of us?'). Some people are eager to know what will happen next, while others are insecure and fearful and refuse to take risks.

After that it was a matter of inventing contrasting characters of both types.

New Brooms

These days there seem to be consultants and advisers and counsellors for almost everything, even trivial problems, and 'How To Do It' books on every subject. This suggests that we are becoming less and less capable of working things out for ourselves, even simple practical tasks.

The idea for this story came to me as I read an

extremely funny review of a serious American television programme on this sort of thing, in which people set themselves up as 'experts' and made a well-paid living out of advising other people what to do and how to act.

From my own experiences as a housewife and mother I had plenty of material to draw on.

The title comes from an old proverb—'A new broom sweeps clean'.

So, here are eight stories, each one starting from its own small idea. When the first 'seed' of an idea begins to grow big enough to become a story, then it is time to start filling out the characters and the plot.

The engaging thing about these 'seeds' is that I'm never quite sure what they are going to grow into or what sort of characters are going to walk into the story. In 'A Bit of a Hitch', for example, when Hatt rang the Zoology Department to find out what baby crocodiles eat, I hadn't planned for tetchy Dr Mangrover to answer the phone. He just did.

Mary Steele